GARY PAULSEN

WORLD OF
ADVENTURE

TRIO

Escape from Fire Mountain

Hook 'Em, Snotty!

Danger on Midnight River

A YEARLING BOOK

Published by
Yearling
an imprint of
Random House Children's Books
a division of Random House, Inc.
New York

This edition contains the complete and unabridged texts of the original editions.
This omnibus was originally published in separate volumes under the titles:
Escape from Fire Mountain copyright © 1995 by Gary Paulsen
Hook 'Em, Snotty! copyright © 1995 by Gary Paulsen
Danger on Midnight River copyright © 1995 by Gary Paulsen

Visit us on the Web! www.randomhouse.com/kids

**Educators and librarians, for a variety of teaching tools, visit us at
www.randomhouse.com/teachers**

ISBN: 0-440-42123-3

Printed in the United States of America

One Previous Edition

February 2006

10 9 8 7 6 5 4 3 2 1

OPM

Escape from Fire Mountain

CHAPTER 1

Nikki Roberts's green eyes flew open. The morning sun was pouring through her bedroom window. She grabbed the alarm clock and frowned. It was Monday and already after seven o'clock. "Traitor. Of all the mornings for you to fall down on your job . . ."

A door slammed downstairs.

The tall blond girl let the clock fall on the bed and frantically pulled on her jeans.

A voice carried from below. "Hurry up, Nikki. We're almost ready." It was her dad, and his voice held a note of impatience.

1

Jim Roberts was a well-respected outfitter and guide in the Wabash Mountains. The family-operated Tall Pines Hunting Lodge functioned as a headquarters for his guided elk hunts. It catered to people from all over the country and was always full in the winter, with a long waiting list.

Now it was off-season. No hunting could take place in the summer, so there were no visitors. Nikki's parents were going to the city, several hundred miles away, for a week to help her uncle Joe, who was recovering from knee surgery.

Nikki had convinced her folks that she was old enough to stay behind and take care of things. After all, she had been raised up here, and at thirteen she was mature enough to remember to feed the stock and keep an eye on the place.

She took the wooden stairs two at a time and found her mom in the kitchen checking for the tenth time a list of things for Nikki to do.

Nikki peered at the list over her mother's

shoulder. "Don't worry, Mom. Everything will be fine. You'll only be gone a few days."

Her mom put the list back on the refrigerator. "I know. But if there *is* a problem, you'll get on the phone and call for help, right? The CB base radio doesn't have the range to get out beyond the mountains."

"She knows all that." Nikki's dad winked at her over the top of her mother's head. He picked up the last suitcase. "You've been over it with her at least a dozen times. Now come on. We told Joe we'd be there before nightfall."

Nikki walked them out to the pickup. Her mom looked around anxiously at the woodland that surrounded the lodge. The river, peaceful and reassuring, tumbled playfully under the log bridge a few yards in front of them. She sighed, hugged her daughter, and got in on the passenger side. "I put Uncle Joe's number right beside the phone."

"I know, Mom. And on the microwave, the TV, and the bathroom mirror. I won't lose it, promise."

Nikki's dad put his arm around her. "Stay close to home, kiddo. No long horseback rides or canoe trips, okay?"

"Dad, you're as bad as Mom."

"Can I help it if I want my head wrangler and chief cook in one piece when I get back?"

"What could go wrong? All I have to do is feed the horses, take reservations, and lie around and eat popcorn."

Her dad stepped into the truck and laughed. "Well, at least go easy on the popcorn." He started the engine. "We should be back by Sunday."

"Good-bye, Nikki." Her mother waved. The truck rumbled down the dirt drive, and they were gone.

Nikki watched them cross over the bridge and disappear down into the valley. A funny feeling of excitement came over her. She picked up a rock and threw it as far out into the river as she could. It skimmed easily across the glimmering surface. Nikki smiled. Then she turned and raced back to the house to begin her first day of independence.

CHAPTER 2

The horses were fed, and there was nothing worth watching on television. Nikki had straightened the entire house, and it was still before noon.

She pulled on her riding boots and wandered back out to the barn. Goblin, her favorite horse, put his head over the corral fence, and Nikki stroked his sleek black neck.

"Dad didn't say I couldn't go riding, you know. He just said not to take long rides." Nikki patted him between the ears. "Anyway, what's long to some people is really not very long to others. Have you ever noticed that, Goblin?"

The horse blinked his big dark eyes at her. She ruffled his ears. "I'm glad you're so agreeable."

Nikki brushed his smooth coat, slid on his bridle, and lightly tossed a blanket on his broad back. She grabbed her saddle, moved to Goblin's left side, and swung it up. When everything was in place, she pulled the cinch tight and stepped up.

In minutes she was heading up the north trail toward Sugar Loaf Ridge. There were some dark clouds in the distance, but it would take a few hours for them to get here. In the meantime, she would take a leisurely ride and check on the elk herd. Then she would come back, make an embarrassing amount of popcorn, and pig out while she watched movies on TV.

Nikki wound her way up the narrow trail, working Goblin into an easy canter. Giant pines lined the trail on both sides. Every so often a rabbit would dart out of the brush and race alongside Goblin, then disappear back into the undergrowth. Goblin whinnied play-fully each time. He seemed to enjoy the game.

Several miles up Nikki topped out on a small peak overlooking a grassy meadow. To her right were beautiful snowcapped moun-tains. It was peaceful here. She stopped and took a deep breath of the fresh air.

In the meadow below a movement caught her eye, and she slid the binoculars from the saddlebags.

Bighorns.

A large band of bighorn sheep was passing through from the salt licks on its way up to the high mountains. The big rams marched like royalty with their curled horns held high. The spring lambs jumped over their mothers, chased one another, and butted heads with an unending supply of energy.

Staying in the shadows of the tall trees, Nikki urged Goblin forward until he was right at the edge of the meadow. Silently she stepped off her horse and tied him loosely to a branch. She slowly crawled closer, using the tall grass for cover.

The lambs were still romping about. One of

the mothers got tired of being hurdled and butted a little one end over end. The tiny lamb tumbled to the ground in a woolly heap. Nikki nearly laughed out loud.

From nowhere a rifle shot cracked the morning and echoed through the valley.

The band of sheep scattered, but it was too late. A large ram fell to the ground.

Nikki froze.

Poachers.

Through the tall grass she watched two camouflage-colored four-wheelers drive up to the ram. Two rough-looking men jumped off and went mechanically to work, slicing and hacking at the throat of the dead animal. They were after its head. Within minutes it was severed. Carefully the poachers wrapped the beautiful curled horns and tied the ram's head on the back of one of the four-wheelers.

Nikki held her breath. No telling what they would do if they found her there as a witness.

One of the men suddenly looked in her direction. He had cold blue eyes and a pointed red beard. She tried to sink lower into the grass. The man began walking right at her. He passed so close he almost stepped on her hand.

A horse whinnied. It was Goblin. He had somehow gotten loose and decided to join Nikki in the meadow.

The man with the red beard grabbed the horse's reins. "Someone's out here, Frank. They probably saw the whole thing."

The man called Frank finished tying the ram's head and wiped the blood off his hands. "Quit worrying. It's just a loose horse. You've been jumpy all day."

The bearded man scowled. "I'll quit worrying when we close down this operation. We've got too much at stake to get caught."

"We're not going to get caught. No one lives in these mountains. There's one old hunting lodge and no people around for miles."

"Then where did he come from?" Red Beard looked at the horse.

"Like I said, he got loose. Probably threw a greenhorn somewhere down in the valley. Give him a swat and send him on his way. We've got more important things to worry about."

The bearded man tied the horse's reins together and hit him hard on the rear. Goblin jumped forward and raced through the trees.

"Don't just stand there," Frank snarled. "Let's get this one back to camp and measure the horns. If it's as big as I think it is, we'll only need three more to fill our order."

The two men climbed on the four-wheelers and drove away, leaving the animal's carcass lying in the grass.

Nikki waited until she could no longer hear their engines before she stood up. Her shoulders slumped. Goblin was nowhere in sight, and it was a good four miles back to the lodge.

Thunder rolled from the east, and lightning crashed behind it. The dark clouds had moved in while the poachers had kept her captive in the grass. Dime-size raindrops started falling.

Nikki shivered, pulled up her shirt collar, and ran.

CHAPTER 3

Goblin was waiting patiently by the barn when Nikki got home. By the time she unsaddled him and made it to the house she was thoroughly drenched. Water ran off her hair and clothes and made puddles on the floor.

The lightning was worse now, striking every few minutes. Nikki looked out the narrow window next to the front door. Another flash popped near the barn, and the ground turned a ghostly white.

Nikki leaned against the wall to catch her breath, wondering what to do about the poachers. "The sheriff," she whispered out loud. Leaving a wet trail, she headed for the kitchen and picked up the phone.

It was dead.

"Oh great." Nikki brushed a piece of long blond hair out of her eyes. She snapped her fingers. "The CB." It didn't have great range, but it would be worth a try.

She ran to her dad's office and had just turned the doorknob when she heard the radio squelch. A garbled voice crackled through the static.

". . . please anybody . . . fire . . . need help, over." It was a child's voice, a boy's, but it shook with fear or pain. "Can you . . . me . . . near the bend in the river. Help us . . . over."

Nikki stayed off the radio, waiting to hear a response, not wanting to interfere with an emergency. There was no answer.

". . . lost . . . fire coming closer . . . anybody hear . . ."

Still no response.

Nikki picked up the handset. *I'll wait a sec-*

ond longer, she thought. *Maybe someone will call him.*

"We . . . help . . . sister's hurt . . . please . . ." The voice was torn by static.

Nikki listened intently, but there were no other transmissions. There would be no help for them.

"I can help you. I'll get you out." Nikki found herself yelling into the microphone. "Can you hear me?"

Except for the buzz of static, the radio was silent.

They hadn't received her.

Nikki tried again. "Can you hold on? Can you tell me where you are? Over."

". . . white rocks . . . can any . . . help us . . ."

The speaker suddenly went dead, as if someone had unplugged the radio.

The poachers would have to wait. Nikki raced upstairs and checked her survival bag. It was always kept packed with dried food, extra clothing, and other gear so that when her father needed her on short notice, she would be ready. She made an attempt to dry off, changed her clothes, and slipped into a raincoat.

By the time she got outside, the weather had begun to clear. The wind still whipped, but the brunt of the storm had moved on.

She started for the barn to resaddle Goblin but changed her mind.

A canoe would be faster.

The boy had described white rocks near a bend in the river. That could only be one place—Deadman's Drop.

The rapids.

Nikki ran to the boat shed and pulled a fiberglass canoe off the rack. She carried it on her shoulders to the water and then went back for paddles and a life vest.

She threw her survival pack in the middle, slid into the canoe, and pushed off.

CHAPTER 4

As Nikki paddled down the rushing mountain river, she searched the horizon for a sign of the fire. Sure enough, a thin gray haze hung just over the top of one of the mountain ridges downriver. She thought she could smell the smoke.

Her dad had been called upon many times in the past to help fight fires in the area, and she had learned that lightning was usually the cause. She was hoping that there had been enough rainfall in that area to keep it from spreading too far.

Nikki breathed a sigh of relief when she

thought about home. The lodge had just received a good soaking. It would be safe for the time being from spot fires.

A loud noise brought her attention back to the river.

She felt it more than heard it. From just ahead came a slow, constant thundering sound.

The first white water.

She reached it in seconds. This small set of rapids wasn't considered too difficult. Nikki had run them many times with her father. Together they had traveled the north fork of the river all the way to Harrison.

Once through, she straightened her back and dropped her knees to the floor of the canoe. Readjusting her grip on the paddle, she began looking ahead for rocks.

The frothing white water tumbled and was loud enough now to block out all other sound as it crashed over the large rocks and curled under in eddies.

The speed of the canoe increased, drawn by the current. The canoe seemed to hang on the edge of a rapid for a second.

Then it shot up.

Nikki could no longer see the river in front of the canoe. Water rolled and splashed over her. The hull grated on a rock. She screamed at herself for not seeing it sooner.

Despite her best efforts to stop it, the stern of the canoe started to turn. In a matter of seconds the small craft whipped around and plunged blindly backward.

She tried to push against passing boulders to turn it back, but the current was too strong.

Then it hit hard.

The canoe scraped its hull against a huge rock and lurched to a stop. A rip could fill the craft with water almost instantly. Nikki quickly inspected it for leaks. She ran her hands over the sides and up and down the bottom, feeling for even the tiniest tear. She found none.

"Okay." Nikki used the paddle to push free from the snag and continued downstream. "Let's get it right this time."

The water in front of her was calmer for the next mile or so. Occasionally the current tugged at her, but she guided the little canoe through with no more problems.

The smoke was easier to see now. It was boiling black from just beyond the next hill.

Nikki let the canoe drift close to shore. The river forked here, and Deadman's Drop would be coming up. She could take her chances and maybe get to the kids faster by trying the dangerous rapids, or she could pull the canoe out now and go overland.

"It won't be faster if I'm dead," Nikki said out loud. She stepped out of the canoe onto the pebbly river bottom and pulled the craft up to the shore, then secured it to a tree with the bow rope.

Quickly she took off her life vest and shrugged out of the thin raincoat. Slinging the pack over her shoulder, she headed toward the smoke.

Nikki wished she had some way of knowing exactly where the boy and his sister were. Since he had mentioned the river, she decided the best thing to do was stay close to it. Maybe they would be waiting somewhere near the rapids.

It hadn't rained here. The brush along the

shore was dry and brittle. There would be nothing to slow the fire. It was free to burn in any direction it chose.

A tangled mass of clawing brush tore at her clothes. She worked through it as fast as she could, the sharp leaves drawing blood from her hands. When it got too thick, Nikki waded in the water to avoid it.

Around the next twist in the river, a wall of pale gray smoke—silhouetted in solid black— rose from the trees just a few hundred yards from her. The underside of the smoke was illuminated in an eerie reddish glow. For a moment she stood transfixed, fascinated in a way she couldn't explain.

Nikki shook her head and bolted blindly through the brush. A mixture of fear and uncertainty flooded over her. One thought ran through her mind: Find the children and make it back to the canoe before the fire cut her off.

She started shouting. "Hey! Are you there? Can you hear me?"

The smoke was a thick black cloud sweeping toward her just ahead of the raging fire. An orange tint settled in the tops of the trees. Nikki tried not to look at it.

She would face the fire soon enough.

"Please, please let me find them," Nikki prayed. She cupped her hands and yelled as loud as her voice could carry, "Where are you? I'm here to help. You have to answer me."

After a few more yards Nikki stopped. She had gone as far as the shore would allow. There was a sheer drop of a hundred feet in front of her. Though she had never been down this fork, she knew exactly where she was.

Deadman's Drop.

The roar from the rapids drowned out her shouting. The air was hot, and pieces of soot flew around her.

Think! Nikki tried desperately to concentrate. *If you were a frightened child trapped in a forest fire, what would you do?*

She stood on the edge of the cliff and watched the crashing white water below.

A tiny hand reached up and touched her shoe.

Chapter 5

Dropping to her knees, Nikki grabbed the hand and pulled a chubby little girl with dark brown curls and big black eyes to the top of the overhang. A boy about eight years old, with the same color eyes and lighter hair, dressed in jeans and a torn green T-shirt, climbed up behind her. He was carrying a toy walkie-talkie.

"What on earth . . ." Nikki stared.

The girl, who looked to be maybe four years old, was wearing a dirty pink jumper. Dried tears stained her cheeks. She sat in Nikki's lap and hugged her hard. "Me and James thought nobody could hear us."

"What are you two doing out here?"

The boy looked sheepish. "It was all an accident. We borrowed my grandpa's canoe, and it sorta got away from us."

"I heard parts of your message on my CB radio and came as soon as I could." Nikki looked them over. "Are you both all right?"

"Molly fell off the cliff and hurt her foot. I don't know how bad it is, but it's all red and swollen. That's how we found that ledge down there." The boy pointed below him.

Nikki peered over the edge. Jutting out from the face of the cliff was a small rock overhang. Far below it the rapids churned violently.

The wind was picking up. Nikki looked behind her. If she had been alone, she would have tried for the canoe, but if she had to carry the girl, it would be next to impossible. The fire had almost made it to the river. The flames were as tall as the trees. They arched, casting a threatening light through the dark, billowing smoke.

Nikki stepped back, gave her pack to the

boy, and picked up the little girl. "We've got to hurry now. James, I'm going to carry Molly on my back. You've got to stay up with me no matter what—understand?"

The boy's dirt-streaked face was serious. He nodded.

Nikki shifted Molly to her back and set out at the quickest pace she could manage and still carry her precious cargo. James stayed right on her heels.

The fire was close, too close. Nikki's eyes were blurred by smoke and sweat. The trees crackled and the wind carried red-hot splinters that singed holes in the children's clothes and stung their skin. Where they stood would soon be nothing but blackened stalks and burned earth. There was only one hope of escape.

Nikki's plan was to get as far away from the fire as possible and then try to go around it. If they managed it, they could rest somewhere for the night and head out for the lodge in the morning—that is, if the wind cooperated and didn't send the fire chasing after them.

As if it could read her thoughts, a sudden

gust of wind blew hot cinders in their direction. A deafening crack split the air and a large tree limb hit the ground in front of them.

Nikki jumped backward, but a tall orange flame licked out and caught her pants leg on fire. She dumped Molly to the side, dropped to the ground, and rolled to put it out.

Slowly Nikki sat up and examined herself. There didn't seem to be any real damage. Her leg was black but not burned and her jeans and sock were only singed.

Molly looked like she was about ready to start crying again. Nikki scooped her up and motioned for James, who was staring wide-eyed, to follow.

"We'll have to be more careful from here on," Nikki said. "But don't worry, guys. There's no way I'm gonna let this old fire get the best of us."

CHAPTER 6

Nikki led her charges down a forest trail away from the fire. "Listen." She searched the tops of the trees. As she did, she stumbled over a tree root and nearly fell. Molly clung to her neck, choking her.

It was getting close to dusk. She put the curly-headed little girl down under a tree, shaded her eyes, and scanned the patches of hazy sky.

The sound drew closer. It was a sort of vibration.

A helicopter.

It came in fast. The rotors whipped and beat the air in a heavy pulse. It was so loud she knew it had to be flying low. Possibly it was a search and rescue team looking for them.

Nikki waved and yelled, hoping to attract the pilot's attention. She grabbed the walkie-talkie from James's hand. "Emergency, repeat, this is an emergency—can you copy?"

The helicopter closed quickly and sounded as if it were coming straight at them. For less than a second she caught a glimpse of its bright navigation lights as it passed directly overhead. Then it disappeared.

Nikki continued to wave and call out, hoping the chopper would circle back and see her. She stared at the gap in the trees, wanting desperately to see the helicopter return. But she knew it wouldn't come back. It was gone.

"Why din't he stop for us?" A big tear rolled down Molly's cheek and plopped on her checked shirt.

Nikki sat under the big tree beside her. "It wasn't his fault, Molly. He just couldn't see us." She took the little girl's hand. "But I don't want you to worry. We're going to be safe."

James knelt beside them. "But we're way up in these mountains. How are we ever going to find our way out?"

"Hey, didn't I tell you not to worry? It may take a while, but I promise—I'll get you out of this."

Molly sniffled and made an attempt to wipe her nose. "I'm hungry."

"I can fix that." Nikki rummaged through her backpack and came up with some trail mix and elk jerky. "Try some of Nikki's special homemade jerky. Actually it's my dad's recipe, but I made it."

While the children ate, Nikki rolled her shoulders and stretched. She hadn't realized until now how tired she was. Molly was small, but after a couple of miles of being carried up and down these hills, she got heavy.

"I'm sleepy." Molly rubbed her eyes with a dirty hand.

"I know you are, but we can't stop here. We have to get as far from the fire as possible before dark."

She handed the toy walkie-talkie back to

James. "Is this what you used to call for help earlier?"

James nodded. "I brought it with us when we left on our trip this morning. I think it's broke now."

"Your trip?"

"Me and Molly got up early before anybody else and took a trip in Grandpa's canoe. We were only going to be gone for a little while. But the river dragged us for miles and miles, and then we crashed on some rocks—"

"It was scary," Molly interrupted. "We almost din't make it out of the water."

"We walked for a real long time," James continued. "Then we saw the fire and started running. That's when Molly fell down on that ledge."

Nikki thought about how lucky the children were. About how Molly could have fallen all the way to the bottom of Deadman's Drop or how they might have been caught on that ledge in a raging inferno. She touched the little girl's ankle. "The swelling seems to be going down. It doesn't look broken. Just badly bruised and maybe sprained."

Even though they were well away from the fire, Nikki was still concerned. The air smelled of smoke, and the wind could change direction at any minute and catch them off guard.

She stood and lifted Molly up in her arms. "We'd better get going. We'll make camp later, when I'm positive we're out of danger."

CHAPTER 7

When it was too dark to see any longer, Nikki pulled a flashlight from her bag, laid Molly down, and covered her up to her chin with dry leaves and grass. The little girl had gone to sleep while hanging on Nikki's back.

It seemed ridiculous to make a fire after what they had just been through, but Nikki knew it had to be done. Temperatures in the mountains dropped suddenly at night, and they had no coats or blankets.

While James collected wood, Nikki cleared a spot for the fire and dug a small hole with her hands. Using pine needles for tinder and matches from her pack, she quickly had a blaze going.

"Move those rocks James and make yourself a bed—like I did for Molly. You'll sleep snug as a bug."

A high-pitched scream ripped through the night.

James jumped. He shivered and moved closer to Nikki. "What was that?"

"I'd say it was a mountain lion." Nikki tossed a rock out of her way, sat down, and pulled dry leaves over her feet. "They sound a lot like people sometimes."

"Do they eat you?"

For the first time Nikki noticed just how scared the boy was. Still, he was trying his best to be brave. She reached over and tousled his hair. "I said I wouldn't let anything happen to you, didn't I? Try to get some sleep. We've got a lot of walking to do tomorrow."

James sat back down. "Do you know where we are?"

Nikki hesitated. "Not exactly. I haven't ever been to this part of the mountains before, but I do have a general idea how far away from my house we are. I figure if we start out early in the morning, we should be home by nightfall. Then we'll call your grandparents and let them know where you are."

"My dad's gonna be awful mad at me. He and my mom were coming to pick us up today."

Nikki shrugged. "Who knows? Maybe he'll just be glad you're safe."

James shook his head. "He told me to take extra good care of Molly while they were gone and not let anything happen to her."

"Then he can't be too mad." Nikki looked at the sleeping little girl. Her chubby cheeks were shiny and pink in the firelight. "I'd say Molly's doing just fine."

James lay back on the ground. "Nikki?"
"Yes?"
"I'm glad you came to help us."

CHAPTER 8

Bright sunlight woke Nikki from a restless sleep. By the position of the sun she could tell that she had slept later than she wanted to. It was midmorning. She rose quickly and poured dirt on the campfire until it was completely out. Then she shook James and Molly awake.

The exhausted group started across the mountain in the direction of the lodge. The trail was rugged. Thick tree roots and fallen branches made every step treacherous. After several hours Nikki pulled the children up a steep rise and called for a rest.

From the top of the high mountain peak they looked down on the blackened forest, still smoking in places. In the center of this once solid green paradise was now a hideously charred scar that stretched for miles. The fire had destroyed the entire face of one hillside and a valley and had then burned itself out at the river.

Nikki knew enough about the mountains and fire not to trust appearances. All it would take was a strong wind, and those smoldering embers could be whipped into another huge blaze.

"Break's over." Nikki stood. Her back and the calves of her legs were beginning to ache. They hurt when she reached down to pick up Molly. "Come on, Little Red Riding Hood, let's hurry up and get through these woods."

Molly giggled. "Are we going to Grandma's house?"

Nikki shook her head. "Nope. We're going to my house. There's no big bad wolf there."

James got to his feet and picked up the

backpack. "How much longer till we get there? Seems like we've been walking forever."

Nikki thought about it. If they continued to cut straight across the mountain, they could be there in a couple more hours. On the other hand, that way would take them dangerously close to the edge of the burn. She studied their faces. They were so tired. Nikki didn't know how much longer they could hold out.

Before she could make the decision, they heard the sound of a small engine. Nikki's face brightened. Firefighters.

"Come on, guys, maybe they can help us."

They ran toward the noise, slipping and weaving through the trees. At the bottom of the hill was a small clearing completely surrounded by forest and hidden from the fire and the world. Tents were set up, and two men were standing in front of them, talking.

"Hello!" Nikki shouted, and waved from the fringe of the trees.

The man with his back to them turned. Nikki stopped in her tracks. It was Red Beard, the poacher. She glanced around the camp. There were rifles leaning against a tree and a beautiful ram's head lying on a piece of plastic on the ground. Two camouflage-colored four-wheelers were parked near the tents.

Nikki swallowed and kept walking. She tried to act as if nothing were wrong. "Excuse me, sir. We're lost, and we were just wondering if—"

Red Beard strode over to them. "What are you doing here?"

Molly peeked over Nikki's shoulder. "We crashed in the water and nearly got burned up. Then Nikki found us, and now we're going to her house to be safe."

The man's piercing blue eyes glowered at the little girl. "And just where exactly is Nikki's house?"

Molly hid her face in Nikki's shoulder. "We're not sure exactly." Nikki moved Molly around to the front and held her close. "Like I said, we're lost."

James touched the curled horn on the ram's head. "Are you guys hunters?"

The other man, the one Nikki remembered as Frank, moved in behind them. He picked up one of the rifles and stood with his feet apart, pointing it threateningly. "Get inside that tent. All of you—now!"

Nikki held Molly with one arm and took James's hand. "Come on, kids. Do what the man says."

There was barely room for all of them to sit down inside the tent. Nikki put Molly on the sleeping bag. Her mind raced. What had she gotten them into? All along she had promised to take care of them, and then, like an idiot, she'd walked right into danger.

She rubbed her forehead and tried to think. These were cruel men—criminals. They had guns and probably wouldn't hesitate to use them.

Molly pulled on her sleeve. "Those men are bad."

"Yes, they are. Very bad."

"What are we going to do, Nikki?" James asked worriedly.

She didn't have an answer for him. They could hear the two men arguing outside the tent. Frank was angry. "I say we get rid of them now, Strecker. No one will know. They'll think the fire got 'em."

"We'll wait. People are probably looking for those kids."

Frank snarled. "All the more reason to take what we have and get out of here before they find us."

"Maybe you're right." Strecker moved away, and they had to strain to hear his voice. "We'll pack everything and leave in the morning."

"What about the kids?"

"We'll take care of them early, before we go."

The tent flap flung open, causing Nikki to fall back with a start. Frank jerked the sleeping bag out from under Molly.

"Sweet dreams, kids." He sneered evilly at them.

"What are they gonna do to us?" James whispered when Frank had gone.

"Nothing." Nikki bit her lip. She felt in her pocket for her knife. "They're not going to get the chance. You and Molly try to get some sleep now. When I wake you, don't ask questions. Just be ready to go."

CHAPTER 9

 Frank had laid the sleeping bag just outside the tent's opening. His sleeping body blocked any escape through the door.

Nikki could hear him snoring. James and Molly were huddled in one corner, using each other for pillows. She pulled out her pocketknife and scooted to the back wall of the tent. Quietly she slit the canvas all the way down, then stepped out and moved around to the front. The moon gave her enough light to see where she was going.

To the four-wheelers.

They were so sure of themselves the men hadn't thought to remove the keys. She unfolded her knife and punctured the tires of one of the vehicles. Then she threw that set of keys into the woods.

Frank made a choking, sputtering noise and sat up. Nikki crouched behind one of the four-wheelers. The big man looked around a moment and then lay back down facing her. In the darkness she couldn't tell if his eyes were open or closed.

She waited for what seemed like hours until she heard his even snoring.

Then she moved to the guns.

One was a high-powered rifle with a bolt. Her dad had one just like it, and she'd seen him use it many times. She slid the bolt out and put it in her pocket. The other gun had a lever action. Nikki felt on the ground for rocks the size of the barrel. With a stick she forced three of them down into it.

Time was running out. Nikki made her way back to the slit in the tent and gently awakened James. "Time to go."

James didn't say a word. He helped her pick up Molly, grabbed the pack, and followed her out of the tent.

They sat Molly on the seat of the four-wheeler, put it in neutral, and pushed it down the valley. They hadn't gone far when Nikki heard yelling. The men were awake and had obviously discovered the empty tent.

"Get on, James!" Nikki put Molly on her lap, turned the key, and pushed the start button.

Nothing.

It wouldn't start. "Come on . . ." She pushed the button again. The machine made a grinding noise and then slowly worked its way into motion.

Nikki kicked it in gear, found the headlight switch, and roared into the forest. She had to pick her way carefully. Even though she had driven her uncle Joe's four-wheeler many times, there wasn't much room to maneuver, and she didn't want to make any mistakes.

Behind them they heard the two men bellowing and cursing over the other disabled four-wheeler. Nikki smiled. Wait until they checked out their guns.

On through the dark night she drove without stopping. After a while James tapped her on the shoulder. "How can you tell which way we're going?"

She pointed at the sky. "Up there. See the Big Dipper?"

"I think so."

"Line up the two stars at the top of the dipper. See that shiny star off to the right? That's called the North Star. You can find your way around at night if you know which direction to travel. Right now we're heading south. And if I don't wreck us, we should run into my house in about a half hour."

CHAPTER 10

 The four-wheeler trembled. Then it sputtered and jerked to a complete stop.

Nikki sighed. "Well, that's it. We must be out of gas. Looks like we walk from here."

James was too tired to say anything. He just climbed off and fell in step beside her.

Nikki was stiff from carrying Molly. She shook out her arms one at a time. Awake Molly was heavy, but asleep she was like a lead weight. Every muscle in Nikki's body screamed at her to stop and rest.

She held the flashlight in the crook of her

arm and kept walking. All the trees and land-marks looked alike in the dark. Undoubtedly they were moving in the right direction, but that didn't guarantee they were heading straight for the lodge. Unless she saw something familiar soon, they would have to turn around and search behind them.

The moon had gone behind some clouds, and it was difficult to see where they were going. Forty-five minutes or more had passed, and Nikki was sure she had somehow missed the lodge in the darkness. It was possible that she had walked right past the house without even knowing it.

Then she heard it. A horse's whinny.

Goblin.

She moved to the sound and in a few yards nearly ran smack into the back of the corrals. Somehow she had managed to lead them to the far side of the lodge. If it hadn't been for Goblin, she might have kept going until daylight.

Nikki headed for the house. She stopped on the front porch. It felt so good to be home.

"We're here."

James was half asleep behind her. His eyes fluttered open. "Is this it? Is this your house?"

"Home sweet home." She hefted Molly onto her hip and led the way into the house. Upstairs Nikki tucked Molly and James into her bed. They were asleep before their heads hit the pillows. Nikki moved for the telephone.

There was still no dial tone, only the soft whisper of static.

The chances of someone's listening to the CB at this time of night were small, but for the children's sake, she plodded into her dad's office and picked up the handset. "If anyone can hear me, we have an emergency at Tall Pines Hunting Lodge. Repeat, this is an emergency."

Nikki called for help until she fell asleep on the desk still holding the receiver.

The big grandfather clock in the hall struck six. Nikki's head jerked to attention. She couldn't believe it. She had actually fallen asleep at the controls.

She tried calling out again. There was still

no response. It was useless. Whatever she was going to do, it would have to be on her own.

Through the window she noticed the horses milling around the water tank. They hadn't been fed the entire time she was gone. "Boy, I'm a fine one to leave in charge." Nikki headed outside to look after them.

Goblin seemed glad to see her. He nuzzled her with his soft white nose. Nikki patted him. "I wish you could help me, boy. Got any suggestions on how to get these kids home? Maybe we'll all pile on you and take off upriver. What do you say?"

"I'd like that."

Nikki turned. James was standing behind her. She smiled. "I didn't expect you to be up yet."

"That clock woke me up."

"Me too." She broke up some hay and threw it into the feeding trough. "Do you ride, James?"

The boy looked down. "No." He glanced up at her. "I sure would like to try, though."

Nikki ran her hand through her hair. "We have a problem, James. The telephone's dead, and I can't pick up anyone on the CB. You and Molly may have to stay with me until Sunday, when my parents get home."

James made a face. "My dad will be worried sick."

"I know. I've been racking my brain, trying to figure out how to get you home."

"Can't you just drive us?"

Nikki was flattered that he thought she was old enough to drive but didn't say so. Instead she told him that her parents had taken the only vehicle except for a broken-down jeep in the barn.

"What about the horses?" James's face was hopeful.

"I thought about that. But the only cabins I can remember anywhere upriver are near Waterton. Is that where your grandfather lives?"

The boy nodded. "We go there every summer for vacation."

Nikki frowned. "Waterton is over sixty miles away, James. By the time we got there my parents would have been back and could have driven you."

"Maybe we could carry gas to the four-wheeler and use it to go home on."

Nikki hadn't thought of that. It was a possibility. The poachers had probably cleared out of the woods by now, worried that their escaped captives had made it to a phone and called the sheriff.

"That's not a bad idea, James. After breakfast we may just give it a try."

CHAPTER 11

Molly bit into a piece of toast. "You're a real good cooker, Nikki."

Nikki laughed. "Yeah, it takes a special talent to pour milk on a bowl of Crunchy Smacks."

"Are we going to take gas to the four-wheeler now?" James asked.

"You finish your breakfast. I'll fill the gas can and go after the four-wheeler. It may take me a while to find it. You and Molly can watch TV until I get back."

James's lower lip went out. "I'd rather go with you."

"I know you would, but Molly needs the rest. Okay?"

He looked at his feet. "Okay."

Nikki patted him on the back. "I knew I could count on you." She squeezed Molly and started out the door. "I'll be back as soon as I find it."

The last thing she wanted to do was take another hike into the woods. But she remembered how good it felt when she finally made it home last night. James and Molly needed to get to their home, too.

The gas can was on a shelf in the boat shed. Luckily it was three-quarters full. She grabbed it and was on her way out when she heard voices.

Through a crack in the door she saw someone in the yard. She pushed the door open a little wider.

It was Frank, and he was carrying one of the rifles.

Nikki drew a sharp breath. She watched him walk around the house, looking in the windows. In a few minutes he was joined at the side of the house by Strecker.

She couldn't make out their words. But she could hear them laugh and saw them move to the porch.

It was easy for them. Frank turned the knob on the front door, and they walked right in. Nikki sank to the floor and closed her eyes. Why hadn't she prepared for this? Anyone with half a brain would have at least considered the possibility that the poachers might find them. Now, because of her stupidity, the kids were alone in the house with criminals.

She tried to gather her thoughts. It was her fault the kids were in this mess, and she would just have to get them out.

She pushed the shed door open barely wide enough to squeeze through. Keeping low, she ran to the barn. Goblin saw her and trotted up.

"I'm gonna need your help, old boy." Nikki slipped a bridle over his ears and saddled him. She led him out the back door into the forest.

Staying in the trees, she circled the lodge and came in behind it. She tied Goblin securely to a branch and moved to the tree line at the edge of the forest.

She watched the house. There was no movement. Nikki took a deep breath. Somehow she had to make it from the trees to the back of the house without being seen. The only way was to run for it.

Nikki hunched over and ran for all she was worth. When she reached the house, her heart was racing—not because she was tired but because she was afraid the poachers might have seen her.

She waited.

No one came out.

Staying close to the wall, she made her way to the bathroom window. It was the only one she knew for certain wouldn't be locked.

As quietly as possible, she slid the window open and pulled herself up and over the windowsill. Again she waited, but no one came.

Nikki swallowed and opened the bathroom door an inch at a time.

Frank and Strecker were in the den. Nikki could hear them talking over the noise of the television. Apparently they were waiting for her to come back. The kids must have told them where she was going.

The carpet muffled the noise as she crawled down the hall on her hands and knees. At the door to the den she sat on her heels and leaned back against the wall. If the criminals saw her, it was all over.

She took another deep breath and peeked around the corner. Luckily the poachers had their backs to her. Molly was watching cartoons, and James was sitting on the sofa, staring at the ceiling.

Nikki waved at him. The first couple of times he didn't see her. The third time his face lit up. He sat up straight and stared at her. She ducked behind the wall.

Frank growled at the boy. "What are you lookin' at, kid?"

James slumped back on the couch. "Nothing." He sat up again. "Mister?"

"What do you want?"

"My sister needs to go to the bathroom."

Molly turned around and looked up at her brother. She was about to protest, but the calm expression on James's face kept her quiet.

Frank's eyes narrowed. "She looks fine to me, kid. Sit down and shut up."

"Okay. But don't say I didn't warn you."

"Let him take the girl to the john," Strecker snapped. "They're not going anywhere."

James took Molly by the hand and started to lead her out of the room. Frank grabbed his arm. "You come right back, squirt, 'cause if I have to come lookin' for you . . ." He drew his finger across the boy's throat. "Got the picture?"

James nodded and moved to the door. Nikki was waiting down the hall in the bathroom. She motioned for them to hurry.

When Molly saw her, she smiled and started to talk. Nikki put her finger to her lips and pulled her inside the room.

She pointed to the window and gave James a leg up. When he was safely out, Nikki handed Molly to him and slid out behind them.

"This way," Nikki whispered. She led them to the tree where Goblin was waiting. "I know you guys don't ride, so listen to me. All I want you to do is hold on tight. Got it?"

"We got it." James helped her lift Molly onto the swells of the saddle. Nikki quickly untied the rope from the branch, climbed into the seat, and pulled James on behind.

"Where are we going?" James asked.

Nikki urged Goblin through the trees. "I don't know. All I know is we have to get away from here."

"There they are!" Frank was pointing and yelling from the bathroom window.

"Hang on." James wrapped his arms around her waist as Nikki moved Goblin into a trot. She held Molly in her lap to keep the little girl from falling while she guided the horse with her free hand.

Chapter 12

Goblin took a long drink of cool river water. Nikki splashed some on her face and then took a drink herself.

James and Molly were playing near the shore. Nikki looked behind her. She didn't hear anything, but this time she wasn't going to take any chances.

Goblin was covered with a white lather. They had ridden him hard and covered several miles. He needed a rest. She decided to let Molly ride while she and James walked for a while.

"Come on, guys. Time to get going." Nikki

lifted the little girl into the saddle. "Hold on tight to the saddle horn, Molly."

James hadn't said a word since they left the lodge, and Nikki was worried about him. "Are you okay, partner?"

He looked up at her. "Do you think they'll find us?"

"Not if I can help it."

"That big man said he was going to use a knife on me if we ran away."

Nikki rested her arm on his shoulders. "You know, James, it just occurred to me that I haven't told you what a big help you've been during all this. I couldn't have done any of it without you."

"Really?"

"Yeah. I don't think those poachers have a chance against us. Together we're too smart for them."

James beamed. "Do you have a plan?"

"Sure," Nikki lied. "There are bound to be people downriver somewhere, making sure that fire is under control. We'll just ask one of them to help us out."

James seemed satisfied with her answer. Nikki wished she were. In an area that big, the chances of running into someone were remote at best.

Goblin stopped walking. Nikki pulled on the reins. He stumbled a few steps, favoring his right front leg, and then stopped again.

Nikki picked up the leg and looked at the underside. The soft frog of the horse's foot had a large thorn in it. She lifted Molly to the ground and jerked the thorn out. Blood squirted from the hole.

There was nothing she could do for him. If they kept riding him, he might become permanently injured. Nikki pulled his saddle and bridle off and put them under a tree.

"You know the way home, fella. When you feel like it, you head on back there." Nikki ran her hand down his neck. She turned and picked up Molly. "I guess you'll have to put up with me now. Goblin can't carry you anymore."

Nikki had just settled Molly on her own

back when they heard something crashing through the brush behind them. She grabbed James's sleeve and pulled him down behind some bushes.

Two of her father's horses galloped by—ridden by Frank and Strecker.

James's face was white. They were going to get caught, and he knew it.

Nikki stood up cautiously. "They'll be back when they lose our trail. We have to stay in the brush and hope they miss us." She looked down the shore. Things here seemed familiar.

Of course. She'd been here two days ago when she had come to rescue the kids. She knelt back down. "James, if it isn't burned up, I have a canoe somewhere nearby. Molly, don't make a sound. We're going to work our way down the shore, and we don't want those bad men to find us."

Walking slowly and staying in the bushes, they moved along the riverbank. They were getting close to the burn, and Nikki was afraid they had missed the canoe.

"There's something." James pointed to some brush ahead of them.

It was the canoe. The fire hadn't damaged it.

Nikki handed Molly to James, ran to untie the slipknot from around the tree, and moved the canoe into the water. "Hurry, kids. Get in."

She slipped Molly's arms into the life vest and reached out to push off.

"I wouldn't do that." Frank's voice boomed from above her.

Nikki looked up—into the barrel of his rifle.

"You've given us enough problems. Step out of that canoe."

Nikki closed her eyes.

And pushed.

The canoe floated a few feet out into the water.

Frank aimed the gun at the canoe and pulled the trigger. There was a moment's hesitation, followed by a deafening explosion.

Nikki looked back. It was awful. Frank lay on the ground covered with blood. She'd never intended for anything like this to happen. Her only thought had been to stop the poachers from hurting the kids.

Strecker ran along the shore after them, screaming threats as he clawed through the heavy brush.

Nikki kept paddling.

CHAPTER 13

Everything they passed on one side of the river was charred and black. On the other side was a vertical rock slab that separated the river's two forks.

Nikki concentrated on her new problem. Deadman's Drop was ahead of them somewhere. The current was swifter now, and it was all she could do to keep the canoe from turning on her.

She needed to get back to shore. But the river had a mind of its own. Every time she got close, the current snatched them and drove them farther out into a crashing torrent.

They couldn't hear anything above the roar of the falls. The shore drew nearer but not fast enough. They smashed into something beneath the water. There was a ripping sound. Nikki looked down and saw a sharp piece of rock tearing through the fiberglass bottom.

The canoe stopped momentarily, then lurched. Water sprayed through the floor, filling the hull. It shot forward and rammed another set of rocks.

Nikki's arms ached. She could hardly move the paddles. The river was winning. It seemed ready to swallow them up.

James yelled at her. She couldn't make his words out above the noise of the rapids. He pointed wildly to shore.

She turned. Forest rangers and firefighters were standing on the bank. They had a long rope and were trying to throw it out to them. Every time they threw, they missed.

The canoe grated on the rocks. Nikki knew it wouldn't stay snagged long.

It started moving again. The current had dislodged it, and the canoe was coming around. The ranger onshore coiled the rope and threw it out.

It was now or never. Nikki lunged for the rope, caught it, and fell into the water. The force of the river drove her into the rocks and pinned her there.

James held a paddle out to her. She wrapped the rope around one arm and reached for the oar. Her fingertips had barely touched it when the river slammed her back against the rocks and down under the water. Her mind carried one thought.

Air.

She broke the surface and took in great gulps. Another rapid washed over her. Everything went dark as the churning water tossed her body about like a rag doll. Just when she thought her lungs would burst, a swell swept Nikki back up.

The little canoe was quickly filling with water. James valiantly held the paddle out to her again. Nikki pushed her exhausted legs against the rocks and stretched as far as possible.

And made it.

Once she had a grip on the paddle, she used it to draw the craft closer to her. When she finally had her hand on the side of the canoe, the men on the bank started pulling them in, heaving until they dragged it into the shallows.

Nikki crawled to shore and fell on the bank. Voices echoed.

". . . the little boy said something about poachers and a gun blowing up . . . we've radioed the sheriff's chopper to pick them up . . . miracle they're still alive . . . find the parents . . ."

The voices sounded hollow and unreal, mixed with the roar of the rapids.

Nikki's eyes opened. The men had wrapped them in blankets. James was sitting on the bank, and Molly was perched on a ranger's lap, listening to his assurances that the sheriff would have the "mean men" in custody soon.

"Are you all right?" One of the rangers handed Nikki a cup of cocoa.

Nikki managed a weak smile and took a long sip. They were better than all right.

They were safe.

Hook 'Em, Snotty!

CHAPTER 1

Bobbie Walker slapped her worn-out cowboy hat against the leg of her faded jeans. It caused a small cloud of dust but she didn't notice. Something else had her attention. Her grandpa's old white Ford pickup was rumbling up the road toward the Rocking W Ranch.

The day she had dreaded was finally here. Bobbie's cousin from Los Angeles was coming to the ranch to visit for a few weeks. Grandpa had left early this morning to go to the airport in Winston—nearly seventy-five miles away.

Bobbie had refused to go along. She wanted

it well understood from the start that bringing Alex out here wasn't her idea. The last thing they needed right now was a city greenhorn getting in the way of the annual wild cow roundup.

The old truck stopped in front of the house. Bobbie pulled her hat down low and moved away from the corrals. She walked to the bed of the pickup and lifted out her cousin's expensive leather suitcase.

The passenger door opened. A tall, slender girl with long brown hair, the same color as Bobbie's, stepped out. Her hair was parted on the side and she moved it off her face with her hand.

Bobbie looked her up and down. She wasn't impressed and it showed. The girl was wearing tight black shorts and a black T-shirt that said PRODUCT OF THE CITY. Bobbie winced when she noticed her cousin's feet.

Sandals.

One side of Bobbie's mouth went up. It always twitched like that when she didn't like something. She barely nodded at the girl and started for the house.

"Bobbie."

It was Grandpa. His voice held a note of displeasure. "Yes, sir?"

The tips of his thumb and forefinger smoothed down his gray handlebar mustache. "I want you to say hello to your cousin Alex."

Bobbie turned. Alex gave her a bored look under nearly closed eyelids. Bobbie shifted the suitcase and halfheartedly stuck out her hand.

Alex folded her arms in front of her. "I wouldn't want you to strain yourself."

Bobbie put her hand down.

"Gramps tells me there's a lot to do out here in the sticks." Alex cocked her head. "What do you do for fun, cousin, wait till Saturday night and count the flies on manure piles?"

"I'm sure Grandpa will find plenty to keep you busy."

"He told me *you* were going to show me around."

Bobbie pushed her hat back. "I really hate to disappoint you, Al, but I'm leaving tomorrow. I'll be gone for more than a week chasing stray cattle in the brush country."

"The name is Alex."

"Like I said, *Alex,* every year, after we gather in the flats, we go up in the hills to look for wild cows."

"Oh gee," Alex mocked, "and I was really looking forward to getting to know you better —cousin."

Bobbie held the suitcase out in front of her and let it drop at Alex's feet. "Yeah, it's too bad there's not going to be time for that."

CHAPTER 2

The next morning Bobbie was up early. Grandpa was already downstairs making breakfast. She took the stairs two at a time and burst into the kitchen.

"It won't work, Grandpa. She's so green . . . you know how it is up there. She won't last a day."

"I told her she could go."

Bobbie could hear the final edge in her grandpa's voice. But she couldn't help trying one more time. "What if she can't ride?"

"She rides. She's been to one of those equestrian schools."

Bobbie knew it was useless. She sighed and headed for the barn. When her grandpa made a decision, that was it. She would just have to get used to the idea of baby-sitting her cousin for the next week. She threw a feed can across the barn and it crashed into the wall above the door.

Alex stepped inside the barn. This morning she was wearing a denim Western shirt over a red T-shirt, a pair of stiff new jeans, and new boots. "Watch your temper there, pard, you nearly hit me." She moved forward and half turned. "Gramps bought them for me," she said, gesturing at her clothes. "How do I look?"

The side of Bobbie's mouth went up but she didn't say anything.

"Gramps said I should come out and see if you need any help."

Bobbie chewed the inside of her lip. "If you're coming with me, you better get ready. I'm leaving in a half hour. I already fed your horse. He's the strawberry roan in the pen. Saddles are in the tack shed."

Bobbie moved past her cousin and grabbed a tarp off a peg on the wall. She took it outside and wrapped it in her bedroll.

In a few minutes Alex returned, leading the roan. Bobbie frowned. The horse's back was still bare. "I told you the saddles are in the tack shed—over there."

"All I could find were Western saddles. I'm used to riding English."

"You mean those itty-bitty things with hardly any leather on 'em and no saddle horn?"

Alex nodded.

"Look, Al, we're not going on an Easter egg hunt. We're looking for stray cattle. Some of them are mean and all of them are wild. You'll be spending whole days in the saddle. Maybe you should tell Grandpa you want to stay here until I get back. It'll only be a week."

"You wish." Alex turned and led the roan toward the tack shed again. "Don't worry about me, hotshot. If you can handle it, so can I."

Bobbie tightened the cinch on Sonny, the big sorrel gelding that was her favorite roping horse. "Looks like we're in for it, old boy." She fastened the saddlebags and headed for the house.

In the yard, she stopped to give Wolf a pat.

He really was part wolf. Bobbie had raised him from a pup and he adored her.

She walked into the house. The screen door slammed behind her. "That you, Bobbie?" Her grandpa came in from the kitchen. "You kids about ready?"

"She's a flake, Grandpa. And besides, she rides English."

"Give her a chance, Bobbie. Look, if they took you to Los Angeles and turned you loose, you wouldn't have a clue. How smart you are depends on what part of the world you happen to be standing on at the time."

The screen door opened. Alex poked her head in. "I'm ready, Wyatt."

"Wyatt?"

"You know. As in—you make me *urpp.*" Alex winked at their grandfather.

Bobbie's face turned red. She thought about dragging Alex outside and settling their feud right then. But one look at Grandpa told her it wouldn't be a wise move. Instead she said, "I guess we're ready, then."

Grandpa followed them out to the horses. Bobbie whistled for Wolf, checked her cinch, and swung into the saddle. "See you in a week, Grandpa . . ."

She looked over at Alex, who was riding the roan in circles, bobbing up and down in the saddle, English style.

Bobbie sighed. ". . . if not before."

CHAPTER 3

The girls rode in silence up a sandy canyon bed for a couple of miles; then Bobbie turned onto a narrow trail to the right. Cattle had climbed the embankment for years and hollowed out a path up the steep canyon wall.

Wolf stayed close. Sometimes they couldn't see him, but he was always within easy calling range.

The path soon became more rugged. Bobbie ducked under a piñon limb that had grown over the trail. It hit Alex full in the face and dragged her off the back of the horse. She landed in the only mud puddle in the whole trail.

The frightened old roan jumped forward a few steps and then stopped, waiting patiently for Alex to get up.

Bobbie turned in the saddle. "Are you okay?"

Alex had a red welt across her cheek. She glared at her cousin. "You did that on purpose." Shaking, she slung some of the mud off her hands, wiped the rest on her pants, and grabbed the reins.

A cow was bawling somewhere down the canyon. Without a word Bobbie sank her spurs into Sonny and loped toward the cliff. The horse lunged off the ledge and landed back in the bottom of a sandy gully with Wolf right on his heels.

Bobbie quickly spotted the cow behind a salt cedar. She was a big cow with a two-month-old heifer calf. Bobbie shook out her rope into a good-sized loop, gave it a couple of twirls, aimed, and let go. The rope landed easily around the calf's neck. Bobbie dallied around the saddlehorn and backed Sonny up a few steps. Then she turned and started up the trail, leading the calf, with the cow following close behind. "Bring 'em up, Wolf."

Alex was back on the roan, waiting in the middle of the trail. When she saw the cow she smirked and said, "Find one of your long-lost relatives?"

"The only relative I have up here is a mud hen, and she's fixing to get run over if she's stupid enough to stay in the middle of the trail."

Bobbie didn't wait for Alex to get out of the way. She pushed past, dragging the calf. The roan pinned Alex's leg against the side of the embankment. The excited cow ran past and kicked backward. She nailed Alex square on the kneecap.

"It's not too late for you to turn back, Al." Bobbie smiled sweetly over her shoulder. "Just follow the canyon down and you'll be fine."

Alex gritted her teeth and tried not to show how much her knee hurt. "Listen, Bobbie, I'm in. Get it through your thick head, there's nothing you can do to get rid of me."

"Why is it so important for you to be up here? You obviously like me about as well as I like you, so what's the big attraction?"

"Maybe it's because I know how much it bothers you that I'm here."

Bobbie shrugged. "It's your funeral." She trotted ahead. The cow and calf had to run to keep up, which meant that Alex had to ride in a cloud of choking dust.

A mile and a half later, they topped out in a meadow completely surrounded by a thick wall of trees. Ancient run-down wooden corrals stood in the middle of the grassy pasture.

Bobbie rode her horse into one of the pens, closed the gate, and let the calf go. She stepped off and led Sonny to the water tank. It was bone-dry. She reached down and turned a valve. Clear spring water gushed into the tank.

"If I were you, Al, I'd water my horse. He's had a long trip." Bobbie let Sonny have a long cool drink.

Alex slid out of the saddle. She walked a bit stiffly and bowlegged as she led the roan to water. Bobbie couldn't help smiling.

"What are you laughing at?" Alex snapped.

"How long have you had it?"

"What?"

Bobbie pointed at her and laughed harder. "Arthritis of the rump."

"I've had enough." Alex let go of her horse and hit Bobbie like a tigress, driving her back and knocking her on her rear. "Now we'll see if *you* have problems with *your* rump."

Bobbie leapt to her feet. Her lips were tight. She stalked past Alex and as she did reached out and shoved her backward.

Into the water tank.

Alex stood up. Her clothes were sopping wet. She shook the water off, pushed her hair out of her eyes, and climbed out. Bobbie was doubled over, laughing.

Alex was steaming. She swung at Bobbie, clipping her on the jaw. Bobbie tried to grab her arm but missed. Alex punched her again, this time in the face. Blood spurted from Bobbie's nose.

The fight was on. Wolf ran back and forth barking furiously as the girls rolled on the ground, each one trying to get a better grip on the other, until they wound up underneath the roan. The horse snorted and danced nervously, trying to avoid them. Suddenly he jumped sideways and came down hard with his front hooves.

Right on Bobbie's ankle.

CHAPTER 4

The orange flame of the fire flickered against the dark night. Bobbie dug her spoon into a can of cold pork and beans. She put some on the grass for Wolf.

Alex studied Bobbie's wrapped ankle in silence. Then she lay back on her bedroll and closed her eyes. "My dad didn't tell me being a cowboy was so much *fun*."

"Your dad?" Bobbie put down the spoon. "I thought he was some kind of bank executive."

"He is, but he used to work this ranch when he was a kid—along with your dad. That's the real reason I'm here. He's always had this big

17

guilt thing about not being around for Gramps when your dad died and he has this stupid idea that somehow I'll suddenly turn into Annie Oakley and make up for it."

"He doesn't need to worry. You're no Annie Oakley, and me and Grandpa do just fine without anybody's help."

"I said it was stupid. Besides, my dad looked into the ranch records. He thinks the Rocking W is about to go under."

Bobbie stared at the fire in silence, then sighed. "Sometimes it gets awful close. That's why I come up and get these strays every year. The money they bring always seems to keep us out of hot water. This year, though, I have to admit, things are a little closer than usual."

"What are you going to do now?"

"What I came up here for."

"How? That ankle is bruised so bad you can't even walk. You're lucky it's not broken. You wouldn't even be over here if I hadn't dragged you."

Bobbie's jaw thrust out. She sat up. "You didn't drag me, you only helped me. I could outwalk you any day of the week." She stopped, then smiled sheepishly, looking at her ankle. "Although you did a good job wrapping up my foot."

Alex shrugged. "You're welcome."

Bobbie used her pocket knife to open a can of peaches. "So, what's it like in Los Angeles?"

"It's great. There's always something going on."

"Like what?"

"Stuff. You know, hanging out."

"Hanging out? Of what, a window?"

Alex frowned. "Are you serious?"

Bobbie stuffed peaches in her mouth. "If you don't want to tell me, just forget it."

"Hanging out is . . . being with your friends. Sometimes we go to down to the mall and just sort of stand around."

Bobbie rubbed Wolf behind the ears. "And you think that's fun?"

"We do other stuff. Sometimes we get into a good game of asphalt football, no rules."

Bobbie stared at her.

Alex stared back. "What? You thought all I did was sit around and paint my nails?" She threw a stick into the fire. "What do you do with your friends, besides all this cowpoke junk?"

"The only kids who live around here are from the Bledsoe place. You passed it coming in."

"You mean that fancy ranch with the two-story house and the white pipe fences?"

"That's the one. They have two boys close to my age but they're both jerks. I keep to myself most of the time. In the summer, I usually break a colt or two, that keeps me busy. Sometimes on Saturday, Grandpa and I go see a movie."

"Sounds kinda tame."

Bobbie eased her ankle up on the swells of her saddle. "We'll see how tame you think it is this time tomorrow."

CHAPTER 5

"Are you sure you can do this?" Alex held Sonny's reins.

"I'm sure." Bobbie stepped into the stirrup on the wrong side of her horse to avoid using her swollen ankle. "Get on your horse. If we see any cattle, I'll do the roping. You and Wolf get behind and push them."

Bobbie led the way out of the meadow through a thick stand of trees. "When we see one she'll probably run. We'll have to move fast or we'll lose her in the brush." She looked back at Alex over her shoulder. "By the way, you're gonna need to learn to duck."

Alex grabbed a pine cone from a nearby tree and threw it at the center of Bobbie's back.

Bobbie shook her rope out and held it close. A flash of black ran across the trail in front of them. "There goes one. Come on."

Sonny bolted after the cow. Trees went by in a blur. The cow was wild and had no intention of letting them come anywhere near her.

They raced over one ridge and started up the next. Alex did her best to keep up. Most of the time she just held on and let the roan decide where to go. The cow made a quick left and the roan nearly lost Alex. Her feet were out of the stirrups and she barely hung on.

Bobbie waited for a clearing. She would only have one chance, and when they exploded out into a small opening she threw her loop. It caught the cow's horns. Sonny stopped dead, and when the black cow hit the end of the rope, she flipped around facing them.

The cow was mad. She fought and pulled and tried to back up. Sonny held her fast. Then the cow made a wild dash around a tree. Bobbie let her fight with the tree until the animal was worn out. Then she calmly rode around the tree and led her captive back toward the meadow.

Wolf and Alex fell in behind. "Are we going to do this for every single one?" Alex asked, breathing heavily.

Bobbie nodded. "Unless you have a better idea."

"At this rate, we'll be up here a month."

"Grandpa and I did it different when he used to come up with me."

"Was it faster?"

"Yeah, but I don't think you'll like it."

"Anything would beat this."

"Cows generally will stick together if you get a few rounded up. If you think you can handle it, I'll go get them and bring them back here to you. Your job will be to keep them together until we have enough to move down to the corrals . . ." She trailed off, waiting for Alex's answer.

"How hard can it be?"

Bobbie smiled mischievously. She pulled Sonny to a stop, giving some slack in the rope. "Take the loop off this one and I'll go hunt you another one."

Alex stepped down and cautiously approached the cow. Alex jerked the rope up and off the horns. The instant the cow was free she took off like a shot.

"Don't just stand there." Bobbie re-coiled her rope. "Go get her. I'll be back with another one in a few minutes. Come with me, Wolf." She smacked Sonny on the rump with the rope and the horse loped off.

Alex scrambled to the roan and climbed on. She could still hear the black cow ahead of her—somewhere—crashing through the brush.

CHAPTER 6

Bobbie was dragging an obstinate bull calf down the trail to the spot where she had left Alex. The calf still hadn't learned that it was easier to follow than to dig in and make Sonny drag him. Wolf nipped the calf's hind leg and then ran back to make sure the mama cow was still following.

Bobbie really didn't know what she'd expected to see when she got back—but she knew this wasn't it.

Alex's red T-shirt was hanging in a tree. It had a big brown arrow on it drawn with mud, pointing west.

Bobbie pushed her hat up and scratched her forehead. "What? . . ."

She grabbed the T-shirt and headed in the direction the arrow indicated. The calf struggled but Sonny was so powerful it didn't matter.

From the top of the next ridge she saw them. Alex and the roan were guarding the entrance to a box canyon just below. Three mama cows with calves were munching on grass in front of her.

Bobbie laughed out loud. "Well, what do you know." She moved down in the canyon and rode up beside the roan.

Alex jumped down and took the rope off the bull calf. She tried to act casual. "We ran across these extras on our way here. I thought we might as well bring them along."

"Amazing." Bobbie shook her head. "I forgot about this box canyon. How'd you find it?"

"Actually, the cow found it. I thought I'd never catch up with her, so I went back and left you that sign." She took the T-shirt Bobbie held out to her. "When I finally found her she was with these others. When they saw me they ran in here and the roan and I trapped them." Alex patted the horse's neck. "We make a pretty good team."

Bobbie snorted and shook her head. "We've been lucky, dumb lucky. But maybe we ought to test our luck by going after Diablo next."

"Diablo?"

"He's a wild bull. And big. Over two thousand pounds. Every year I go after him but so far he's always managed to get away. One year he hooked my horse, nearly killed him." Bobbie showed her the scar on Sonny's shoulder. Then she looked her cousin in the eye. "If we could get him, he'd be worth a lot."

Alex shrugged. "I'm game."

"Okay. But if I manage to bring him in, it'll be your job to keep him."

CHAPTER 7

"Get out of the way!"

Alex could hear barking, and pounding hooves coming at her. She pushed the roan close to the canyon wall.

Bobbie and Wolf shot past her. Seconds behind them was the ugliest, meanest-looking animal Alex had ever seen in her life. The bull was enraged and obviously bent on destroying Bobbie.

Bobbie jerked Sonny up short behind a boulder. The bull stopped, snorted at Wolf, pawed the ground, and prepared to charge.

Alex put two fingers in her mouth and

blew. The whistle pierced the air. The bull raised his head and looked around. For the first time he noticed the cows standing off to the side. He looked back at Bobbie, bellowed, and blew snot on the ground. Then he turned and trotted over to inspect the herd.

"I thought *you* were supposed to bring *him* in. Alex led the roan to the boulder. "Looks like it worked the other way around."

"That was close." Bobbie wiped sweat off her forehead with her sleeve. "Thanks for distracting him."

Alex's eyes widened. "Do my ears deceive me, or did I just hear Bobbie Walker say thank you?"

Bobbie ignored her. "I surprised Diablo in the brush just up the trail. He didn't care for it much and started after us. Figured if he was going to chase me anyway, I'd lead him back here."

Alex looked over at the big bull, which was now standing quietly with the rest of the herd. "How do we convince him to go with us to the pens?"

"As long as he's with the cows, we won't

have much trouble from him. But don't crowd him. We'll edge around and start them out of the canyon. Then I'll move up to the side. You and Wolf stay behind and push them out. Just remember—take everything nice and slow."

CHAPTER 8

They had fourteen head in the pen, including Diablo. Bobbie was trying to put the enormous bull in a separate pen. Both girls were still on their horses, trying to cut the bull out and force him into the next corral. Wolf had been ordered to stay out of the way.

"Try to get around on the other side. Work them easy. Careful, don't get too close to him." Bobbie shouted instructions as she moved around Diablo.

The bull snorted and pawed the ground. He ran straight at Sonny. But the big sorrel had played this game before. He quickly side-stepped and let the bull go past into the other pen.

Before the bull realized what had happened, Alex jumped down and pushed the gate shut behind him. She wiped the sweat and dirt off her face and leaned tiredly against the gate.

"Man, am I glad this day's over."

Bobbie looked at the sky. "We still have some daylight. Better stay after it till dark."

"You're not thinking of going back up there and finding more cows tonight, are you?"

"No. We've got plenty to do right here. Those calves need branding, and we ought to go ahead and castrate that bull calf and de-horn that one over there." Bobbie pointed across the pen.

Alex wasn't listening. She had her back turned and was watching Diablo. The bull's eyes were blood-red and he was still snorting and running around in circles.

"My dad told me people used to actually ride those things."

"What? Bulls? They still do. Mostly in rodeos now, though." Bobbie glanced over at Alex. "I've tried it a couple of times."

"Get real."

"I have. At the Fourth of July Rodeo. It's really not so bad. Hittin' the ground is what hurts."

"Are you serious? You couldn't get me on something like that for a million bucks."

Bobbie nodded. "I understand. You have to have backbone to ride bulls."

Alex's eyes narrowed. "What do you mean by that?"

"Nothing. It's just that you gotta be tough to ride bulls, that's all."

Alex stared through the wooden rails at Diablo. "You did it?"

"Sure."

Alex climbed up on the gate. "You rope him. I'll get on him."

"Hey, I was talking about normal bulls. This one's loco. He'll kill you."

Wolf growled. The hair on his back was standing up. A deeper voice cut the evening air. "Yeah, Bobbie. And we wouldn't want the new little girl hurt, now would we?"

Bobbie turned. Two boys were sitting on horses looking down the side of the hill at them.

"Calvin and Jesse Bledsoe," Bobbie said, her voice flat. "What are you two doing on Rocking W land?"

Jesse, the older and meaner Bledsoe boy, sneered. "It's a free country, Walker." He rode his gray horse to the corral fence and peered over it at the cattle. "Some of our cows have turned up missing and we thought they might have wandered over here. We're just checking."

"If we run across anything of yours we'll send it back your way."

"I just bet you will." Calvin, the younger boy, who was about Bobbie's size, spit a wad of tobacco juice on the ground. The brown liquid dribbled down his chin. "After you stamp the Rocking W brand all over them."

Bobbie forgot about her swollen ankle. She flew over the fence and pulled Calvin off his horse. Before the boy had time to react, Bobbie was sitting on his stomach and had his arms pinned to the ground.

Jesse started to step off his horse.

"I wouldn't do that if I were you." Alex pointed to Wolf. The dog was snarling and baring his teeth.

Bobbie let Calvin up and dusted off her jeans.

Alex moved to the top rail of the fence. "I'm new at all this cowboy stuff, but if I see either one of you around here again, I'm gonna let Wolf have you for supper. Understand?"

Calvin picked up his hat and glared at Bobbie. "This ain't the end of it, Walker."

The two boys mounted, wheeled their horses, and rode off. When they were out of sight Bobbie turned to Alex.

"Let Wolf have them for supper?"

Alex shrugged. "I read it in a book. It worked, didn't it?"

Bobbie couldn't help smiling. "Yeah, I guess it did."

CHAPTER 9

"This is crazy. Besides, it's fixing to rain. We better get the tarp out and make a tent or we're going to get wet."

"In a minute." Alex was balancing on the top rail of Diablo's pen. Waiting.

"I don't know how I let you talk me into this. I'm going to get my rope off of him and get ready for the rain." Bobbie started to climb the fence.

"Get back. Here he comes."

The bull had been mad about being penned up. But he was even madder now that he had a rope around his neck and two humans were practically in the pen with him. He charged at the fence. Alex saw her chance and jumped, landing squarely on his back just to the rear of his shoulders.

For a split second the bull was so surprised he didn't move. Then suddenly his temper flared and he went wild. Alex barely caught the rope before Diablo started bucking.

There was nothing else to hang on to. Alex clenched her knees as tight as she could, closed her eyes, and held on.

The bull was infuriated. He pitched up and down, sideways and around. But Alex managed to stay with him.

Bobbie couldn't believe it. She waved her hat in the air. "Yee-haw. Hook 'em, snotty! Stay with him, Alex. You got the old booger beat."

Then it ended. In a beautiful arc Alex flew through the air.

Into the water tank—again.

The bull turned and started for her. Alex tore up the fence and fell over the other side.

She was breathing hard when Bobbie got to

her and pounded her on the back. "You're a natural, cousin. Best ride I've seen in a while. And that dismount was something else."

Alex took in air.

Bobbie waited until Alex was breathing normally again and walked her to the camp. "You were great. A lot of first-time riders throw their guts up. Really, one time I saw Toby Matlock throw up for a half hour. It was gross. He musta had spinach for lunch because it was all slimy and green. . . ."

Alex held her stomach, gulped, swallowed. "You're not helping things here."

Thunder rumbled and Bobbie looked up. The clouds were black. The rain would be here any second. She quickly moved the saddles under a tree and covered the bedrolls with the tarp.

A drop hit Alex on top of the head.

Bobbie motioned for her to get underneath the tarp. "We don't have time for a tent. We'll be dry enough under here."

"Speak for yourself. You're not the one who just went for a swim in the water tank."

When the rain came it was as if someone

had tipped over a huge bucket of water. The two cousins moved down in their bedrolls with Wolf snuggled in between. They held on to the edges of the tarp so that it wouldn't blow away.

"Bobbie?"

"What?"

"Next time I start to do something that stupid, I want you to—"

Lightning crashed and Bobbie couldn't hear the rest of Alex's request. She grinned to herself and went to sleep.

CHAPTER 10

The rain stopped about mid-night and all the clouds were gone by morning. Except for the wet grass and mud, it was as if it had never happened.

Bobbie pushed the tarp back and peeked out. Wolf licked her face. The sky was bright and blue overhead. She stood up and stretched.

She stopped. Something wasn't right, some sound was missing. She turned to the corral.

The cows were gone.

She ran to the pens. The gate was down, trampled in the mud.

Alex came up behind her, still rubbing the sleep out of her eyes. "I guess the lightning spooked them."

Bobbie moved inside the first pen. "That's what they wanted us to think."

"They? What are you talking about?"

"The Bledsoes. They did this."

"How can you tell?"

"The cattle might have run through the gate all right, but Diablo didn't open his own pen and follow them. Look over there."

Alex turned to look where Bobbie pointed. Diablo's pen was empty and the gate was standing wide open. "Those morons. Hadn't we better go after them?"

"On what? They took our horses."

Alex looked at the grassy hill where Bobbie had staked the horses the night before. They were gone too. All that was left were the girls' saddles and bedrolls.

Alex rubbed her hands together as she thought. "You know this country better than I do. Where do you think they took them?"

"It doesn't matter. We can't go after them on foot."

"Why not? Your ankle seems better this morning. Besides, we don't have horses in L.A. and we manage to get around." She moved to the saddles, untied Bobbie's saddle-bags, which held the food, and slung them over her shoulder. "You in or out, cowgirl?"

Bobbie ran her hand through her hair. She let out a deep breath and then whistled for Wolf. "I thought you told me to stop you when you wanted to do something stupid."

"They're your cows, aren't they?"

Bobbie nodded.

"You said the ranch might go under if you don't get them, didn't you?"

Bobbie nodded again.

"Then what's stupid about it? We need to go get them."

Bobbie untied her rope from the front of her saddle. "How can anybody argue with logic like that?"

CHAPTER 11

"Are you sure you know where you're going?" Alex leaned on a nearby boulder.

Bobbie sat beside her. "Like I said, it's a shortcut."

"I hope it beats your last shortcut."

"Give me a break. How was I supposed to know that canyon would be full of running water? I didn't know it had rained that hard up here."

"How soon before we get to this 'Turkey Roost,' anyway?"

"Not long. Just over the next ridge."

"What makes you think that's where the cows are?"

"The Bledsoes wouldn't take them home because it would be too easy for them to get caught. They're not smart enough to think of using the box canyon. So that leaves the Turkey Roost. It's the only other place on this whole mountain with even a piece of a fence that will hold cattle."

Alex stood up. "If we're that close, let's get going."

Bobbie's shoulders drooped. Her ankle was starting to throb and she noticed that her breathing was a little ragged. "I can't remember the last time I walked this far."

"That's because you're spoiled. Every time you step out of the house you probably jump on a horse."

Bobbie thought about telling Alex a thing or two about being spoiled. Then she remembered the morning she had actually tried to do her chores while riding Sonny. She half smiled and decided to save it for another time.

"Listen." Alex held up her hand. "Do you hear that?"

Wolf's ears were up. He was alert and started for the next ridge.

Bobbie called him back. She tried to get a grip on her breathing. "It's the cattle. They're bawling because those idiots have them penned up with no water."

Alex stayed low and climbed to the top of the ridge. She could see the cows. They were in a small clearing just on the other side of some trees. Diablo wasn't with them. The Bledsoe boys had made camp and were sitting near the fire laughing about something.

Bobbie crawled up behind her. "I don't see the horses or the bull."

Alex worked her way around a stand of pine trees. She motioned for Bobbie to follow and pointed to a spot on the other side of the cattle. "The horses are over there. They're not even tied up." She spoke in a low voice. "They must not be too worried about us coming after them."

"They need to start worrying." Bobbie squared her shoulders and headed down the hill.

"Hold on." Alex grabbed the back of Bobbie's shirt. "We need a plan."

"Why? Aren't you the one who said they were my cows and I should just go get them?"

"If you go rushing down there, who knows what those two might do? They could turn the cattle loose and we'd wind up chasing them all over again."

The corner of Bobbie's mouth twitched furiously. "I know one thing, we're not going to get them back by standing around here talking about it all day."

"Right." Alex picked up the saddlebags and moved under a tree and sat down. She rummaged inside and pulled out a can of tomatoes. "Yechh. Don't you eat anything besides beans, peaches, and tomatoes?"

"You're going to eat at a time like this?"

Alex nodded. "Those guys aren't going anywhere. Besides, it will give us time to make our plan."

CHAPTER 12

"This idea of yours better work." Bobbie stroked Wolf as she put her arm through the coiled rope.

"At least in the dark we have the element of surprise on our side."

They stood on the hill above the Bledsoes' camp. The fire had gone down to a dull glow. Both boys seemed to be asleep in their bedrolls. Alex could hear them snoring all the way to the top of the ridge.

The cousins made their way silently down the hillside and found their horses' halters and lead ropes in a heap next to a tree stump where the Bledsoes had tossed them. Bobbie handed Alex the roan's halter and moved to untangle Sonny's.

Alex slipped the halter over the roan's ears. The old horse seemed glad to see her. Alex patted him and scratched his neck.

They untied the Bledsoes' horses and pushed them gently away into the brush, then slipped Jesse's and Calvin's saddles onto their own mounts. Working silently, in a short time they were ready for the cows.

Across the opening, in the pale moonlight, Alex could see the Bledsoe boys still sleeping. She saw something else too.

Their boots.

Quickly she dismounted and tiptoed to the bedrolls.

Bobbie tried to grab her as she went past but Alex was too fast.

One pair wasn't enough. Alex reached for the second pair.

A large hand clamped around her ankle.

She fell forward.

The older Bledsoe had her foot. She twisted and threw the boots at him, pounding him in the chest and face. Jesse loosened his grip and Alex scrambled to stand up. He tackled her. The air blew out of her lungs. She felt as if someone had dropped a house on her.

Calvin sat up, reached his hand down the back of his long underwear, and scratched. He squinted out into the darkness. "What's going on, Jesse?"

"Get over here and help me, stupid. She's getting away!"

Alex squirmed out from under Jesse and managed to get to her knees. Calvin kicked off his sleeping bag and reached for her arm. She swung wildly with the other one.

Calvin yelled and held his eye. "She hit me!"

Bobbie rode up with Wolf by her side. The big dog snarled menacingly. "What do you think, Alex? Is it suppertime for Wolf?"

The boys froze as the dog neared them. Alex looked up. Bobbie was sitting on Sonny, laughing. She struggled to her feet, threw her hair back, and glared at Bobbie. "It took you long enough."

Bobbie smiled. "Yeah, I thought I better

bust this up before one of these poor boys got hurt." She turned to the Bledsoes. "Seems we have a small case of cattle rustling going on here." She rubbed her chin. "If I remember right, that's still a hanging offense."

"Want me to get a rope?" Alex asked.

Jesse shook his head nervously. "We were just having a good time with you, Bobbie. You know that. Shoot—we ain't no rustlers."

"Maybe we'll just let the sheriff decide about that, Jesse. Although it looks like a pretty clear-cut case to me."

Calvin looked worried. "Our dad will kill us if you call the law. He's running for county commissioner next month."

Alex moved beside Bobbie. "Maybe you clowns should have thought about that before you stole our cows."

"Our cows?" Jesse looked confused. "Who are *you*, anyway?"

Bobbie laughed. "Boys, I'd like you to meet another Walker. And in case you haven't figured it out yet—messing with her was probably the biggest mistake of your lives."

CHAPTER 13

Bobbie crawled out of her bed-roll the next morning to see Alex already saddling the horses.

"Too bad we lost Diablo," Alex said.

Bobbie shrugged. "There's always next year."

"Maybe we should stay up here a few more days and look for him."

"Naw. We better get these cows on home. Grandpa will start to get worried if we stay up here too long. And besides, we probably need to let somebody know about them." Bobbie pointed to a big pine tree. On either side was a Bledsoe, still dressed in his long underwear and tied securely to the trunk.

Jesse strained against the ropes. "You can't leave us here, Walker. There are bears up here."

"Don't worry," Alex yelled, "one sniff of you and they'll run the other way." She leaned close to Bobbie. "What are you really going to do with those two?"

"I figured we'd start the cows down the trail a ways and then I'd come back and untie them later."

Alex looked over at the boys. "Sure you don't want to go ahead and hang them?"

"It's tempting, but I guess I'll pass."

Alex pulled the barbed-wire gate open and the cows started filtering out. She stepped up onto her horse and began working to keep them bunched.

Bobbie watched her as she cut left to keep one of the calves from turning back. "Say, Alex, I was just wondering . . ."

Alex trotted closer. "What was that? I didn't hear you."

"I said I was just wondering about something."

"What?"

Bobbie cleared her throat and her mouth started twitching. "I was just thinking that if you weren't doing anything next spring . . ."

Alex's face broke into a grin.

CHAPTER 14

 Bobbie leaned down from the saddle and pulled the mailbox open. She took out a handful of letters and shut the box. One was postmarked Los Angeles. She ripped it open.

Dear Bobbie,

Just a line to let you know I made it home okay. I told my friends all about you and we're agreed. You should break one less colt this summer and come out for a visit. I told them it wasn't your fault that you were a just a hick from the country and made them promise not to be too rough on you.

Of course you realize it might not be as exciting as watching flies on manure or going to a movie on Saturday night, but we'll see what we can do.

Seriously, I would like to see an old cowpoke like you try to stand up in a pair of Rollerblades. So let me know.

Alex

P.S.

By the way, what does "hook 'em, snotty" mean anyway?

Bobbie folded the letter and stuffed it inside her shirt pocket. "Shoot, Sonny," she said, "everybody knows that's what you yell to a rider before he mounts a bull." She smiled, remembering the sight of Alex on Diablo's back. "So what do you think, Sonny? Want to go to California and hang out?"

The big horse shook a fly off his neck.

"I know what you mean." Bobbie moved him into a slow lope. "On the other hand, maybe you and I *should* go on out there. We'd show those city slickers a thing or two for sure."

GARY PAULSEN
ADVENTURE GUIDE

RIDING

A horse is a large, strong, and beautiful animal. But remember, a horse is not a plaything, and it can hurt you. Always stay by the front half of a horse's body, even when grooming or mounting. Never make any sudden movements. Horses scare easily.

Equipment is very important to riding. Your saddle should not only fit you comfortably, it should also fit your horse, leaving it free from *gall,* or rub marks. A bit should suit your skill and your horse's mouth. Reins should be made of a material you feel comfortable handling.

Mount your horse from the left side, remembering to stay well away from those back hooves. Place your left foot in the stirrup, hold the reins in your left hand, grab the saddle horn, and step up. Throw your right leg over the saddle.

Gather your reins in one hand. Leave enough slack so that you are not bearing down hard on the horse's mouth. To go forward, gently nudge the horse with the heels of your boots. To back up, pull the reins evenly straight back toward the saddle horn. To turn right or left, simply pull the reins in the direction you want to go. Make sure you are sitting up straight. Your heels should be down.

If you are an inexperienced rider, practice riding your horse at a walk in an enclosed area. Later you can move up to a faster gait. When you are finished with your ride, be sure to give the horse a good rubdown.

ROPING

Roping is a challenging test of technique and accuracy. There are more than a hundred different brands and styles of ropes. Beginners should choose an inexpensive nylon rope. Shake the rope out in the store and see how the loop hangs. If it's lopsided, don't buy it.

Start by practicing roping on the ground. If you're lucky enough to have a plastic steer or calf head that you can stick in a bale of hay to use as a target, great. If not, you may have to choose something different. Fence posts or bicycle handlebars work just fine. (Little brothers and sisters do not!)

Coil your rope from the straight end. If you are right-handed, hold the end with the loop in that hand, with your index finger pointed. Let the coils rest loosely in your left hand. (If you are left-handed, do the opposite.) Shake your loop out a little larger than your coils.

Twirl your loop over your head in a flat, circular motion. Point your index finger at the target and throw the loop as if you were throwing a rock. The coils should slide through your left hand. When the loop settles around the target, pull out the slack.

One important reminder: Horses can be dangerous. Do not attempt to rope from horseback unless both you and the horse are experienced.

Danger on Midnight River

CHAPTER 1

Daniel Martin took one last look around his bedroom. It was pointless to put it off any longer. With a sigh he grabbed his suitcase, threw his sleeping bag up on his shoulder, and slowly walked outside.

The front screen door slammed behind him. He stood on the porch, ran his hand through his short brown hair, and looked up at the dark clouds in the sky. If he was lucky, there would be a storm and the whole dumb trip would be canceled.

He thought about his mom. He knew she

1

wouldn't be able to come and see him off. She was working. She was always working.

Daniel's mother was the day-shift waitress down at the Corner Cafe in town. It had taken her a year of scrimping and saving to get together enough money to send him to Camp Eagle Nest in the Premonition Mountains. This trip was so important to her. She said she wanted Daniel to have some fun for a change.

Daniel didn't want to go to any stupid camp. It wasn't that he didn't appreciate his mom's hard work, but he would rather have spent this summer the way he had every other summer since his dad had died five years earlier—in the Rocky Mountains with his uncle Smitty.

Uncle Smitty didn't treat him the way everyone else did. Up in the mountains it was understood that Daniel could take care of himself. He had spent a lot of time listening and learning about things that might mean the difference between life and death.

Daniel sighed again. That was another

world. In this world—this town world—he was his mama's baby boy. He was thirteen years old, but she insisted on driving him to school and kissing him goodbye every morning.

School wasn't much better. At school he was the class nobody. They called him things like nerd face and dork breath. It wasn't his fault he was a slow learner. For some reason, he just couldn't understand things as easily in school as when Uncle Smitty taught him stuff at the cabin. The teacher called him a student with special needs. Most of the kids called him retarded.

Daniel rounded the corner by the gas station in the center of town and looked up. His lanky frame stiffened. *Wouldn't you just know it? The Eagle Nest van is already here. The driver's probably one of those cheerful types who'll whistle and make jokes all the way to the camp.*

For a second he entertained the thought of going to the cafe and telling his mother that he'd missed the van. But knowing her, she'd work twice as hard so that she could get off early and drive him the seventy miles to the stupid camp.

No, he'd just have to tough it out. Uncle Smitty had told him it probably wouldn't be that bad. He'd said to try and have fun with it. *Fun—at a rich kids' camp for snobs. Sure, no problem.*

The driver was standing by the back of the van when Daniel walked up. "You're late, squirt. Give me your gear and let's get this show on the road."

Daniel shrugged and handed him his suitcase. *So much for the cheerful type.*

The large man practically ripped the sleeping bag out of Daniel's hand. "I said let's go, kid. I don't get paid by the hour. This is my first trip as a driver for the camp and I don't want no foul-ups." He shoved the boy toward the sliding side door of the van.

"Well, well. Look who's here. Daniel the dork."

Daniel paused on the second step and looked up into the pudgy face of Scotty

Howard. His worst nightmare had just come true. Scotty and his friends Troy Dennis and Brandon March were the only other passengers in the van.

Troy was big for his age, with an attitude to match. He looked out the window. "Where's your mama, Danny boy? Ain't she gonna come down and kiss you bye-bye?" Troy and Scotty howled with laughter.

Brandon let his feet slide off the seat in front of him. They hit the floor with a thud. His dark blue eyes narrowed and he scowled. "Leave him alone, boneheads. Let him get in the van."

"Aw come on, Brandon." Scotty held his hands out. "We're just trying to have a little fun with the geek."

"Later." Brandon's face was serious.

"Whatever you say, O wise one." Scotty moved out of the aisle to let Daniel pass. As Daniel took a step, Scotty stuck his foot out and tripped him. Daniel fell to his knees.

He jumped up with his fists clenched. "Try that again, lard bucket."

"Not in my van." The driver growled as he pulled the sliding door shut. "You peacocks can fight all you want after you get there. For now find a seat and sit in it. Don't even think about getting out of it before we get to the camp." Climbing in behind the wheel, the driver turned toward them. "I also don't want no music, loud talking, or snoring." He mumbled something under his breath about spoiled rich kids and started the engine.

Daniel moved to the last seat at the back of the van. He propped himself in the corner and pretended to go to sleep.

Scotty sat down in the seat in front of Daniel and whispered, "I wouldn't sleep too soundly, Danny boy. You never know when the boogey man might get ya."

Troy and Brandon spun around in their seats two rows ahead. Troy laughed. "Watch it, Scotty, you're scaring him. We may have to stop and get his teddy bear out of his suitcase."

Brandon rubbed his eyes and took a pack of

cards out of his back pocket. "Why don't you idiots grow up?"

Scotty leaned back over the seat. Daniel could feel the boy's hot breath on his face. "You're gonna love camp, Danny boy. I'm gonna see to it personally."

CHAPTER 2

The storm was steadily growing worse. Giant drops of rain pounded the van with a vengeance. The driving wind buffeted the van and made it hard to stay on the road.

Daniel stared anxiously out the window. They had been driving in the mountains for several hours. He looked at his watch. They should have been there by now.

He glanced at the three boys laughing and playing cards in the middle of the van. They were acting as if they didn't have a worry in the world.

The driver was a different story. Beads of sweat dripped off his forehead. His knuckles were white from clutching the steering wheel so hard. Daniel could tell that the man could barely see the road, and more often than not the van veered over onto the shoulder.

Abruptly the van left the pavement and began traveling on a dirt road. Daniel looked at his watch again. They hadn't passed a car in more than an hour. He considered asking the driver if they were lost, then decided against it. If they were, there wasn't anything Daniel could do about it anyway.

From the hollow sound the van made as it passed over the wooden planks, Daniel could tell they were on some sort of bridge.

The driver scratched his head and muttered under his breath. "Don't remember no bridge out here. Musta made a wrong—"

Suddenly it felt as if they were flying. The plank noise was gone and the van soared effortlessly through the air.

When it hit the water, it hit hard. The boys were thrown against the walls like rag dolls.

The van was instantly sucked into the raging current and dragged downstream.

The driver was hanging limply over the steering wheel. Blood trickled from the corner of his mouth. Outside, the rain still hammered down. The heavy front end of the van was completely submerged, and only the back stuck out of the water as the churning river drove it down the treacherous canyon.

Daniel opened his eyes and shook his head. It felt as if he'd been kicked by a mule. His forehead throbbed and he could feel a knot on it. He raised himself up and tried to see outside. The back end of the van was slowly sinking.

There was only one chance. Crawling to the back door, he unlocked it and pushed it open. The rain pelted him and the wind forced him back. He braced himself and shoved.

It was an immediate fight for his life. The angry water hurled him down the river as if his body were no more than a stick.

Daniel was a strong swimmer, but the swift-moving current was too much for him. It was all he could do to keep his head above the surging water. A couple of times he thought he heard someone yelling. But for now he had his own problems. The river was freezing cold, and it offered no way out.

CHAPTER 3

Branches clawed at his face and clothes. He reached up and locked his right arm around one. The current yanked his legs underneath the tree. Daniel held on. With what little strength he could muster, he inched his way up the tree trunk to the bank.

The rain had turned to drizzle. Daniel lay on the bank exhausted. It was getting late, and he was chilled to the bone. He didn't know how long he'd lain there before he finally opened his eyes. More than anything he would have liked to stay there and rest, but a nagging voice inside his head was telling him he had to keep moving. It was cold and there was a risk of hypothermia.

Daniel pulled himself into a sitting position and surveyed his surroundings. In front of him was the river. It was dangerously high, with no apparent way back across. Behind him and up the short canyon bank was forest as far as the eye could see.

The rain had soaked almost everything in sight. Building a fire to dry out would be quite a trick, even using everything Uncle Smitty had taught him. Daniel moved up the mountain a few yards away from the river. Sitting under an evergreen, he dug through the wet, dead leaves until he found some dry needles and a couple of dead branches.

He carried them up the hill and sat down under a large tree that had branches thick enough to protect his precious tinder from the drizzle. Reaching into his pocket, he drew out a pocketknife and cut away the outer bark of the dead branches until he had completely dry wood. With his hands he dug until he had a fire pit. He arranged the dead leaves and needles in a teepee shape.

Daniel took a deep breath. *So far so good.*

Going back to the bank, he walked up and down until he found a good-sized piece of chert, a shiny black rock. He scooped it up and ran back to his campsite.

Holding the rock near the dead needles and wood shavings, he struck it with the back of his knife blade. Sparks flew, but nothing caught.

Seven times he tried before a tiny spark ignited the end of a dead needle. Daniel blew gently until there was a small blaze. Then he added more wood shavings and finally a branch.

He left the fire to search for more wood. When he had enough to keep the fire going for a while, he took off his shoes and socks and put them close to the flames to dry.

He leaned back against the mountainside with his toes toasting near the fire. Its warmth felt good. He was almost asleep when he heard it.

Yelling.

He sat up on one elbow. Before, he had been so worried about himself that he had completely forgotten about the rest of the van's passengers.

The thought of going out in the rain again made Daniel shudder. But he knew it was the right thing to do. He built up his fire, then slipped on his damp socks and shoes and stepped out from under the protection of his tree.

The yelling was coming from downriver. The van must have passed him while he was lying on the bank. He ducked his head and trotted to keep from getting chilled again.

About fifty yards downriver he found them. The current had slowed and lodged the van on some boulders near the middle of the river. Only a small piece of the van's white top showed above the water.

Scotty was lying half out of the water, coughing and vomiting on the rocky bank. Brandon was frantically swimming around the van, trying to get a door open.

When Scotty saw Daniel, he pointed at the van. "Troy! He's still in there!"

Daniel didn't hesitate. He kicked off his shoes and jumped into the water. When he got to the van, Brandon screamed, "Troy's hurt but he's still alive! The door's stuck and I can't get him out!"

Daniel dove under the water. He tried to pull the back door open, but it was wedged tight against a rock. He quickly swam to the side door and rammed his shoulder into it. It moved, but not enough.

Daniel held on to the mirror and kicked the door. It popped open. He went to the surface for a quick gulp of fresh air and then dove back down.

Inside the van he saw the driver still hanging lifelessly over the steering wheel. Daniel searched for Troy and found him floating at the top of the water near the back of the van.

Daniel's lungs felt as if they were about to burst. He grabbed Troy under the arms and worked his way out the door. Holding on to

17

Troy with one hand, he fought his way to the surface.

"He's not breathing," Daniel said between gasps. "He'll need mouth-to-mouth. Help me get him to shore."

CHAPTER 4

 Daniel built the fire up until he had a roaring blaze. He had put Troy as close to the fire as he dared, hoping it might help to bring him around.

Troy was breathing, but he was still unconscious. His skin was light blue, and he was shivering. Daniel rubbed Troy's hands and arms. He turned to Brandon. "Dig down under that tree over there and bring me all the dry leaves, moss, or grass you can find. And hurry."

Brandon didn't question him. In a few minutes he returned with an armful of dry leaves and grass. Daniel began stuffing them inside Troy's clothing and packing them around him. "It'll help insulate him from the cold."

Daniel continued to rub Troy's feet and legs. When Troy's socks were dry Daniel put them back on him. He felt Troy's forehead. It was hot.

Scotty looked a little better and was now resting against the huge tree watching Troy anxiously. "Is he gonna die?"

Daniel didn't look up.

"Is there anything I can do?" Brandon asked.

"You can get us a supply of wood. The main thing is to keep him as warm and dry as possible."

"I can help." Scotty started to stand.

"You take it easy." Brandon pushed him back down. "I'll get it."

Scotty watched Daniel work. "How do you know all this stuff? I mean I've seen you in class. You're no Einstein."

Daniel shrugged. "Most of what I'm doing is

just common sense. Besides, Brandon's the one who did the mouth-to-mouth."

Troy moaned softly. His eyes opened. "Where . . ."

Scotty moved to him. "It's okay. There was an accident. The van fell in the river. Danny boy here pulled you out."

Troy looked over at Daniel. His mouth turned up in a feeble grin. "Thanks."

"I was in the neighborhood."

Brandon came back with an armload of wood. "Hey. Nice to see you in the land of the living again. I thought there for a minute you were gonna check out on us."

Troy coughed. "Me too."

Daniel shook out his handkerchief and headed for the river.

"Wait up." Brandon jogged up to him. "Where you going?"

"Troy's still not out of danger. He needs hot liquids." Daniel dipped his handkerchief in the water until it was dripping wet and quickly ran back to the fire. He held it over the flames until it was warm.

Daniel told Troy to open his mouth, and he let the warm water drip in until he had squeezed the handkerchief dry. Then Daniel stood up to repeat the process.

Brandon took the handkerchief. "I'll do it this time."

The two boys took turns until Daniel was satisfied that they had done all they could. He felt Troy's forehead again. It wasn't quite as hot.

Daylight gave way to darkness, and the only light came from the fire. The rain started up again, but the boys were fairly well protected under the branches of the big tree.

Scotty and Troy were sleeping soundly. Daniel added a good-sized stump to the fire so that it would burn all night, then cleared a place to stretch out.

Brandon threw a handful of pine needles into the fire. "You're okay, you know."

An awkward silence filled the night. Daniel stared into the flames. "Most people are—if you give them half a chance."

CHAPTER 5

Brandon sleepily yawned and opened his eyes. It was midafternoon and the sun beat down on him. He sat up and stretched.

A small fire was still burning. A large rock with a hollowed-out center sat near the edge of it. Something liquid was boiling in it. To the side of the fire was a generous pile of pinecones.

Scotty and Troy were still asleep. Daniel was nowhere in sight. Brandon shook Scotty's ankle. Scotty turned over and opened one eye. "What?"

"Wake up. It's the middle of the day."

Scotty rubbed his eyes and sniffed the air. "I'm starved. What's cooking?"

Brandon shrugged. "I don't know. Daniel must have left it. Looks like water with chopped-up pine needles in it."

"It's tea." Daniel stepped out from behind a tree. The front of his T-shirt was filled with round green berries.

He dumped the berries on a grassy spot. "It's made from pine needles. Has more vitamin C than orange juice." Using his handkerchief, he tipped the rock and let some of the liquid run into a piece of bark he had carved out with his knife. He held it out to Scotty. "Try some."

Scotty took the bark. "I'm game." He sipped the hot liquid. "Not bad."

Brandon picked up one of the pinecones and tossed it into the air. "What are we gonna do with these? Have a war later?"

"Those are part of your breakfast." Daniel held one of the cones over the fire. When it was warm he easily popped off some of the scales. "See these little winged-looking seeds?" He put them in his mouth. "They're good."

"These don't taste all that great." Daniel pointed to his little cache of berries. "But they'll help fill the empty place in your stomach."

Scotty stripped off a few of the berries and tossed them in his mouth. "Danny boy, you are amazing."

A small rock flew through the air and hit Scotty in the chest. Troy sat up and smiled. "You dummies gonna keep all the grub to yourselves or what?"

Scotty threw the rock back. "I think I liked you better when you were unconscious."

Daniel poured some of the tea for Troy. Troy reached for it, and some of the leaves and pine needles fell out of his shirt. He looked at Daniel. "Would it be okay with you if I unstuffed myself? I feel like a scarecrow. This junk is kinda uncomfortable."

Daniel nodded. "I don't think you need it anymore. But you still ought to take it easy today."

"Does that mean you think we should wait another day before we try finding our way out of here?" Brandon asked.

Daniel nodded again. "Troy wouldn't get too far before we'd have to stop and make another camp, and besides"—he looked up at the sky—"it's a little late in the day to start."

Scotty popped some scales off his pinecone. "Why don't we just stay where we are? Someone's bound to find us sooner or later. Until they do, Troy can rest up."

"They don't know where we are." Daniel poured more tea for Troy. "The way I figure it, the driver took a wrong turn about an hour out of town. After that he just kept going. We should have been at Camp Eagle Nest two hours after we left yesterday, but we were still driving after about four hours."

"You mean we're not even close to the camp?" Scotty's voice rose slightly.

Daniel shook his head. "We could be anywhere. I think the driver knew we were lost and he kept trying different roads hoping to get back on course."

"What are we going to do?" Troy asked.

"We have three choices. One is to sit here, build a signal fire, and wait. We can hope someone sees it and comes to get us. The second is to walk up this side of the river to the place where the bridge washed out and see if the road leads anywhere."

"What's the third thing?" Brandon asked.

"The third thing is the most dangerous, but if it works it'll get us home the fastest. We go downstream and find the slowest-moving part of the river and try to get to the other side. Follow the river back upstream to the bridge and then follow the road home."

"Not me." Troy shook his head. "Ain't no way this boy is getting back in that water. Forget it."

Brandon looked at Daniel. "Which way do you want to take?"

"Back across the river."

Chapter 6

 Several hours later Daniel dropped his wood by the fire. It was strangely quiet around the camp. Scotty nudged Brandon with his elbow.

Brandon cleared his throat. "We, ah, we took a vote while you were gone."

Daniel was silent.

"It's just that we think it makes more sense to stay on this side of the river. I mean, it's safer and that road on this side of the bridge has to lead somewhere, doesn't it?"

"We don't want to go against you or anything, Danny boy." Scotty looked sheepish.

"We appreciate everything you've done and all, but Troy's a little nervous about the water, and to tell you the truth, so am I."

Daniel knelt by the fire. He didn't look at them. His voice was low. "What if it doesn't lead to anything? It could just be an old forest road the rangers use to check on things up here."

"We think it's worth a try," Brandon said.

Daniel stood and wiped his hands on his jeans. "Maybe it's for the best. If we split up, one of us is bound to find help sooner or later."

"We don't necessarily have to split up," Brandon said. "Unless you want to."

"Like I said, it's probably for the best."

Troy touched Daniel's shoulder. "No hard feelings?"

Daniel shook his head. He looked up at the night sky. *Well, at least I was the hero for a little while. I should have known these guys didn't really want me around. To them I'm still Daniel the nerd.*

Scotty punched him in the arm. "As soon as

we reach civilization we'll come looking for you, Danny boy. Promise."

Daniel put a log on the fire. He stretched out on the ground and turned over so that they couldn't see his face.

"Right," he said quietly.

CHAPTER 7

Daniel sat on his heels and watched the water. He had walked downriver for more than two and a half miles, until he'd found a likely-looking spot at which to cross. He had been watching it for a long time. It didn't look too deep, and the current appeared to be slow enough that he could get across without too much trouble.

He thought about the three boys back at the camp and how, for a little while, things had been different among them. For the first time he could remember, Daniel had actually felt like part of a group. Then they had turned on him.

They had all been asleep when he had silently withdrawn this morning. He had purposely left early so that he wouldn't have to face their empty goodbyes.

Daniel looked at the sky. Dark clouds were forming to the east. It would probably rain before afternoon. He smiled. With any luck, he would be halfway home before it hit.

Still, he didn't move to cross the river. He knew he was stalling. His thoughts kept going back to the trio on the mountain. He doubted they even knew how to start a fire.

Why should I care? Daniel suddenly stood up and stepped out into the water.

He stopped and thought of what his uncle Smitty would say about his leaving three helpless boys stranded on the mountain.

On the other hand, there's really no rush. Maybe I'll just hang around up here for a while.

"You and your big ideas." Brandon paused and looked around them. "Some shortcut,

Scotty. We've been walking for hours, probably in circles. Why do I ever listen to you? We
should have crossed the river like Daniel
said."

"Nobody stopped you." Scotty was breathing hard. "You weren't too anxious to swim
across that river last night."

"That's because last night I was dumb and
listened to you two. Daniel knows what he's
doing. Didn't you see him? He fed us and kept
us dry. Not to mention the fact that he saved
Troy's life."

Troy sat on a log. "Let's take a break. I'm
beat. We can argue all we want but it doesn't
help our situation. We're lost." A drop of rain
the size of a quarter hit him on the nose.
"Great. This is all we need."

"Come on." Scotty led the way through
the brush. "We need to get under a tree like
the one Daniel found, before we get
soaked."

As if on cue, the heavens opened and un-
leashed a furious downpour. Before they
could take ten steps it was raining so hard it
was difficult to see where they were going.

The boys crashed through the brush and dove under the first big tree they came to.

The only problem was, the space under the tree happened to be occupied. The little striped animal stamped its feet and hissed in warning. Then it whirled and in a flash sprayed them with foul-smelling liquid.

Scotty got the worst of it right in the face. He screamed and ran back into the rain, holding his hands over his eyes in pain.

Brandon grabbed Scotty's arm and pulled him to another tree Troy had found a few yards away. They huddled together near the base of the tree while the wind blew sheets of rain at them. They were helpless. There was nothing to do but cover their heads and wait the storm out.

CHAPTER 8

 Daniel sat back and took a sip of his rainwater tea. The rain was beginning to let up. When it was clear enough he would try to pick up the boys' tracks again. Strangely, Brandon, Troy, and Scotty had left the river and cut across the mountain. Their tracks had led him over the tops of two ridges. There was no telling how far they had gone before the rain had hit.

He felt edgy. The newspaper was full of stories about backpackers who had lost their way up here. The Premonition Mountains were famous for catching inexperienced hikers unaware.

Daniel had never hiked up here. He didn't know these mountains at all. But thanks to the time he had spent with his uncle, he knew there was little chance of his losing his way.

He wished he could say the same for Brandon and the others. *What are they doing?* In the direction they were going they would never cut across the bridge road.

The air was cool, but he was anxious to get started. Taking handfuls of dirt, he doused the little fire. He knew it would be next to impossible to find any tracks after the rain. The best he could hope for was that the boys would continue in the same direction and break off branches here and there, leaving a trail that he could follow.

It was slow going. He circled and circled, hoping to find some sign of where they had gone. The noise he was making startled an old doe. She jumped out in front of him and bounded away.

Daniel smiled. *Some backwoodsman. I'm louder than a herd of buffalo.*

The doe drew his attention to some brush off to his right. The bushes had been trampled recently and hadn't had a chance to recover. Daniel pushed some of them aside. Under one was the clear imprint of a tennis shoe, now filled with muddy water.

He looked in the direction the boys appeared to be heading. It didn't make sense. Why would they try to cross the Premonitions —unless they were lost? If they were, it would make his job even harder. They could change direction at any time.

Daniel wondered if he had made a mistake. Maybe it would have been better for him to cross the river and get help instead of wandering around up here. He cupped his hands and yelled for the others.

There was no answer.

He decided to keep going. If he lost their trail now, he might never be able to find them.

When the van didn't show up at Camp Eagle Nest, he figured, they'd send out search parties. A lot would depend on how wide an area they covered. The searchers wouldn't be able to spot the van at all now. On his trip downriver he had discovered that it had completely sunk below the surface.

Anyway, he doubted if a search party would think to look on this side of the mountain range. The more he thought about it, the more he was convinced that the driver had taken them close to a hundred miles in the wrong direction.

Daniel worked the area carefully. He cut their trail again near an ancient pine tree. The dirt and pine needles under the tree had been packed down. He studied the place where the three boys had waited out the rain, and scratched his head.

The tree was on the wrong side of a small ravine. They had been sitting facing the wind as it drove the heavy rain in at them. To stay dry, all they would have had to do was move to a tree on the other side of the ravine, or move around to the other side of this tree.

These guys are worse off than I thought. They don't even have enough sense to come in out of the rain.

From the tree, the tracking became easier. The boys had walked in the mud and left a good clean trail. Daniel followed it up a rocky slope. From there they had taken a ninety-degree turn and moved parallel with a rock cliff.

Daniel paused at the top of the cliff and looked out. Below him was a sheer drop. In front of him were miles and miles of forest. It was a forbidding sight.

The possible urgency of the boys' situation jarred him back to reality. It was getting late and he still hadn't been able to catch up with them. Which meant they would probably spend a cold, sleepless night without food or water.

Part of him felt as if they deserved it. But another part remembered the way Brandon had defended him in the van, and the look on Troy's face when he'd tried to thank Daniel for saving his life.

He kept going.

Chapter 9

Brandon was awake. He had dozed fitfully but had been awake most of the night. His T-shirt was still damp from yesterday's rain. And he still had no idea where they were. Slapping his arms to warm himself, Brandon looked at the sky. "Come on sun."

Scotty squinted up at him. "You couldn't sleep either?"

Brandon shook his head. "Too cold. How're your eyes?"

"They still sting. But that's not what's keeping me awake. I'm starving. I've been trying to

43

get these stupid pinecones to open up, but they won't."

"Daniel said you have to hold them over the fire. And since we don't have one . . ." Brandon looked around. "Where's Troy?"

Scotty rubbed his eyes. "He said he had to go to the john."

"How long has he been gone?"

"Come to think of it, he's been gone a pretty long time."

Brandon cupped his hands. "Troy!"

There was no answer.

"Come on." Brandon helped Scotty to his feet.

Scotty stumbled after him. "You don't think he's lost, do you?"

Brandon just looked at him.

"Right," Scotty said.

Brandon moved along the cliff yelling Troy's name. "Wait." Brandon stopped. "I think I hear something."

A muffled voice came from below the cliff edge. "Help me! I'm down here!"

Brandon ran to the edge and looked over. "Troy, what happened?"

Troy was sitting on a rock ledge a few feet below. His leg didn't look right. It was thrust out to his side at an odd angle.

"I stepped wrong and the whole world fell in. I think I busted my leg. Lucky for me this ledge was here or I'd be a goner."

"Can you move it?"

Troy shook his head.

Brandon searched for a way down. Though the distance was only a few feet, there wasn't one. "Scotty, you hold my feet. I'm going to hang down there and try to pull him up."

"Are you crazy? I can't hold both of you."

"You got any better ideas?"

"I do." Daniel stepped out onto the cliff.

The boys turned. Relief washed over Brandon. "If there was ever anybody I was glad to see, it's you."

Scotty squinted at him. "Is that you, Danny boy? I thought you'd be halfway home by now."

"And miss all the fun?" Daniel looked over the edge of the cliff. "How's the weather down there?"

Troy gave him a halfhearted grin. "Don't tell

me. You just happened to be in the neighborhood, right?"

"Something like that." Daniel turned. "You guys hand me your belts."

Daniel pulled his belt off, tied it to the other two, and jerked the slack out of them. He handed one end to Brandon. "Lie down and hang on to this. Scotty, you hook your foot around that bush and hold Brandon's feet."

Holding one end of the belt rope, Daniel scooted to the edge of the cliff and lowered himself to the ledge below.

One look at the angle of Troy's leg told him it was broken. Daniel shook his head. "Some people will do anything for attention."

"I'd be real happy to share this kind of attention, believe me."

Daniel moved around to stand behind Troy. "There's only one way to get you out of here. I'm going to help you stand on your good leg. Then grab the belt and Brandon and Scotty will pull you up. Ready?"

Troy nodded.

Daniel bent down, lifted Troy under the

arms, and helped him hop to the belt rope. "No matter how much it hurts, you have to hang on, okay?"

"You're the boss." Troy took the end of the belt rope in both hands.

Daniel motioned with his thumb. "He's ready. Pull him up."

Inch by inch Brandon pulled. The jagged rocks tore at Troy's flesh and ripped his clothes, but he hung on. When they got him to the edge, Brandon grabbed his arm and dragged him up and over the lip of the cliff.

"Okay, now me," Daniel called. He was easier to pull up because he could help with his legs. When he reached the top he went over to Troy and felt his lower leg. "You really did a job on this. Hang on, I'll be right back."

Troy's face was white from the pain. "I'll be here."

Daniel moved off the rocky slab and found two sticks about the same length. He tore a strip off the bottom of his T-shirt and trotted back to where Troy was lying.

"This is going to hurt some."

Troy gritted his teeth. "Do what you have to do."

Daniel straightened the leg as gently as he could. Troy winced and drew a sharp breath. Daniel put a stick on either side of the leg and wrapped them in place with the strip from his shirt.

"That's the best I can do for now."

He tied the last knot, then moved upwind and sat on the rock slab. "I hate to mention this, but you guys really stink."

Scotty stepped around Brandon. "We had a little run-in with a skunk last night."

"Smells like the skunk won."

Brandon rubbed the back of his neck. "We kinda made a mess of things. I don't suppose . . ."

Troy raised himself up on one elbow. "What he's trying to say is, since you left we haven't had anything to eat and we don't have a clue where we are."

"How about it?" Scotty asked. "Want to get three hardheads out of the woods?"

Daniel stood up and brushed off the back of his jeans. "If we're going to get out of here, it's going to take all of us." He looked at Troy. "Especially since Troy has decided he'd rather ride than walk."

CHAPTER 10

Daniel directed the building of a makeshift stretcher. They found two long branches and pulled the smaller limbs off. Using their belts, their shoelaces, and strips off their T-shirts, they tied shorter branches across the two longer ones.

Daniel filled in the cracks with pine boughs. He made a mock bow in front of Troy. "Your carriage awaits." Scotty and Brandon lifted Troy from the ground and carefully placed him on the stretcher.

Daniel intended to stick to his original plan and cross the river at its slowest-moving point. He checked the sun and started back in the right direction. The boys took turns carrying the stretcher throughout the day. Daniel gathered edible grasses and berries, and they ate as they walked.

When it was nearly dark, Daniel motioned for them to set the stretcher down under a tree. Troy's face was still white. His eyes were closed and he was obviously in pain.

"Sorry I can't offer you anything to drink." Daniel cleared a place for a campfire. "But tomorrow we'll be at the river and you can drink your fill."

Scotty lay back in the dirt. "I'm done. I don't think I can walk another step."

"How long will it take us to get home after we get to the river?" Brandon asked.

Daniel blew on twigs and pine needles to start the fire. "It depends on how long it takes us to get across and how far it is back upriver to the washed-out bridge."

"I heard something." Scotty sat up. "It's coming from over there." He pointed out into the gathering darkness. "There it is again. Something's in that brush."

Brandon sat up. "Bears?"

Daniel moved behind the fire and picked up a sturdy round stick.

A large brown dog trotted out into the opening. He stopped when he saw the fire and the boys.

"Oh, it's just a mutt." Scotty held out his hand. "Here, boy."

"Don't call him." Daniel eyed the dog. "Everyone stay perfectly still. Don't give him any reason to come this way."

The dog lowered his head and growled. He took a step toward them and hesitated.

Brandon cautiously reached for a stick. The dog snarled and bared his teeth. White foam dripped from his mouth.

Troy felt around on the ground beside him. His hand rested on a large rock.

The dog pawed the ground like an angry bull. He shook his head and some of the white slobber flew off. For a minute it looked as if he was going to turn and go back into the bushes.

Suddenly he charged straight for them, lunging at Daniel. Daniel quickly sidestepped and brought the stick around. He nailed the

53

dog on the back of the head, knocking him to his knees.

Troy raised his rock and brought it down squarely on the dog's head. The dog didn't move. Daniel stepped closer, his stick still raised.

The dog wasn't breathing.

Daniel poked it with his stick. "You got him, Troy."

"I don't understand." Scotty looked bewildered. "Why did he act like that?"

Daniel moved back to the fire. "Rabies."

Brandon pointed his stick at the dog. "He could have killed us."

Daniel nodded. "If he had bitten one of us, we probably wouldn't have lasted more than a couple of days."

Scotty was still staring at the dog. "I wonder what he's doing way out here?"

"No telling." Daniel put a piece of wood on the fire. "He probably made it to this side before the bridge washed out, picked up the disease, and couldn't figure out how to get back."

Scotty nervously looked out into the darkness. "What if he bit something else?"

"He probably did. That skunk you guys told me about, for instance. Skunks don't usually roam around in the daytime unless something's wrong."

A shudder went through Scotty. "This place gives me the creeps. The sooner we get home the better."

CHAPTER 11

When they reached the river, Daniel made them boil the water before he let them drink, to eliminate any possibility of contamination from diseased animals. Then they drank until they thought they would burst.

After a short rest, they carried Troy downstream until Daniel found the place where he had wanted to cross.

Again Daniel sat and watched the water, searching for any telltale signs of drop-offs or other hidden dangers.

"What are you waiting for?" Brandon came up behind him. "It looks okay to me."

"You're probably right, but it never hurts to check." Daniel threw a rock into the water. "You and I will make sure Troy gets across and we'll let Scotty worry about the stretcher, okay?"

"Sounds like a plan to me."

Daniel stood up. "Let's get started."

Brandon and Daniel lifted Troy off the stretcher while Scotty slipped it out from under him. Scotty wrapped his arm around the first rung of the stretcher and stepped out into the water.

Daniel looked at Troy. "All you have to do is float. Brandon and I will do the rest."

Scotty shouted at them from the middle of the river. "I'm still standing. It's not that deep here."

"Hear that, Troy?" Brandon patted his shoulder. "Piece of cake."

They stepped down into the water. Daniel moved to the lead and put his arm under Troy's chin to keep Troy's head up. Brandon stepped to the side to help push Troy through the water.

"Sure beats swimming." Brandon looked down at Troy. "We're almost there."

Daniel turned to look back at them. As he did, he stepped into a bottomless hole. He lost his hold on Troy and sank below the water. Brandon reached for Daniel to pull him back up.

The current grabbed Troy. The upper part of his body was floating away. Troy's leg was useless, so he tried to use his arms to swim. He splashed frantically, trying to get turned around. Brandon snatched at him and managed to hang on to Troy's shoe for a second, but it quickly slipped out of his hand.

Daniel broke the surface of the water and gasped for air. He swam wildly in Troy's direction and grabbed the front of his shirt. "Gotcha."

Troy hung on to him. His voice trembled. "I thought you guys said this would be a piece of cake."

Brandon helped turn him around.

"We lied."

CHAPTER 12

"I see it. There it is."

The boys had made it to the bank and were following the river back to the bridge. Brandon pointed excitedly. "We found it," he announced to the others.

Daniel and Scotty followed him up a rise. They laid Troy down and walked to the bridge. Now that it wasn't raining, it was easy to see that part of the bridge was missing. There was a gaping hole in the center. The three boys looked over the edge and stared at the swift-running water below.

"It's amazing any of us are still alive."

Scotty looked downstream. "It's too bad about the driver. I wonder if they'll ever find his body."

"They'll find him." Daniel stepped back. "When we get back we'll give them the approximate location of the van. It probably hasn't moved that much. It was stuck pretty good."

Daniel reached for his end of the stretcher. "We better keep moving, it's getting late. With any luck we could run into a car sometime tomorrow."

Scotty sighed and picked up his end. "The first thing I'm going to do when I get back is take a long, hot soak in the tub."

Troy raised his head. "I'm going to the hospital—and after that I'm going to have the biggest cheeseburger in town."

"I'm going to fall into my water bed and sleep for a thousand years." Brandon looked at Daniel. "How about you? What's the first thing you're going to do when you get back?"

Daniel looked embarrassed. "First I'm going to make sure my mom knows I'm all right." He glanced up at Scotty. "She kinda worries about me. Then I guess I'll go home and call my uncle Smitty and tell him all about our time up here."

Scotty shifted the weight of the stretcher. "There's something I've been meaning to tell you, Danny boy." Scotty hesitated. "All that stuff I said earlier. You know that stuff on the bus about your mom—well, I was being a jerk."

"Me too." Troy smiled. "But Scotty was the biggest jerk."

"You won't get any argument from me." Brandon thumped both of them on the back of the head.

Two tiny lights flickered in the distance. They moved closer.

"I see it, but I don't believe it." Daniel moved to the center of the road. "It's a truck."

The headlights grew larger until a light-green truck stopped in front of them. A forest ranger stepped out. "By the looks of things, I'd say you boys must be the lost campers."

Brandon clapped Daniel on the back. "Are you kidding? Daniel here knew where we were all the time."

The ranger helped them put Troy in the bed of the truck. "Looks like you had a rough time, son."

Troy shook his head. "Naw. Not with Daniel around. He's the one who set my leg."

The ranger looked at Daniel. "Sounds like these guys were lucky you were along."

Scotty stepped up. "We probably wouldn't have made it without him."

The ranger smiled. "There's a reporter from one of the big papers waiting back in town. I'm sure he'll be very interested in how you boys survived the Midnight River."

"Reporter?" Scotty slid into the front seat with the ranger. "Did I say we wouldn't have made it without Daniel? What I meant to say was that I was a big part of getting us out alive. Yes sir. A very big part." Scotty was still talking as he slammed the door.

Brandon looked at Daniel and shrugged. "So he's still a jerk, what can I say?" He jumped up into the back of the truck. "With friends like us, you'll have to stay on your toes."

Daniel stepped up into the truck bed. He

looked through the window at Scotty, who was still talking the ranger's ear off. Troy and Brandon were discussing what a pain Scotty was.

Daniel wasn't really listening. He had stopped at the word *friends*. . . .

GARY PAULSEN
ADVENTURE GUIDE

RIVER SURVIVAL

Always study the movements of any stream or river you are about to cross. The current in the middle of a river is faster than the current closer to the banks. But even next to shore, chances are the current is not flowing evenly. Try to locate eddies (areas of backward-flowing water), rapids, or bottomless holes, which could trap you.

If you become caught in swift-moving water, turn on your back with your feet pointing downstream to deflect rocks or other obstacles. Keep your legs up; do not attempt to stand. Watch for branches or logs that you can grab on to to keep you afloat. If the water calms, turn on your side and swim for shore.

Get out of cold water as fast as you can, and take every measure possible to get warm. The threat of hypothermia is real. Hypothermia is a condition in which the body temperature drops below normal and heat is lost faster than the body can produce it. Symptoms of hypothermia include slurred speech, blue or white skin, and uncontrollable shivering. To combat hypothermia, raise the body's temperature by sitting near a fire, drinking hot liquids, wrapping the body in warm clothing, or stuffing dry leaves between the skin and damp clothing.

If you must cross unfamiliar water, do not cross at a certain place simply because it is where your path meets the river. Take time to seek out the safest place to cross.